# The maske[barcode: D0446564]

Mack Bolan staggered backward, lining up his sights on his opponent. Before he could draw a bead, the man was on him, grabbing the pistol. Bolan hit the earth with a breath-stealing thump, his gun flying from his hands. His opponent jumped on top of him and settled on his chest, crushing the air out of his lungs.

Just as Bolan's vision began contracting to a fuzzy gray tunnel, his hand scrabbled over the other man's mask and found his unprotected throat. Curling his fingers, Bolan threw a short punch directly at his enemy's Adam's apple. Taken by surprise, the man choked. His grip slackened for a moment, and that was all Bolan needed.

Twisting his upper body, he wrenched the merc's hands from his throat and shoved him off.

Bolan rose first.

Tackling his opponent, he slammed his interlaced fingers into the back of the man's neck.

The merc collapsed to the ground, with the Executioner on top of him, and lay there, unmoving, as one last breath wheezed out of him.

# MACK BOLAN ®
## The Executioner

# The Executioner®
### Don Pendleton's®

## JUNGLE HUNT

## A GOLD EAGLE BOOK FROM
# WORLDWIDE®

TORONTO • NEW YORK • LONDON
AMSTERDAM • PARIS • SYDNEY • HAMBURG
STOCKHOLM • ATHENS • TOKYO • MILAN
MADRID • WARSAW • BUDAPEST • AUCKLAND

Recycling programs
for this product may
not exist in your area.

First edition April 2012

ISBN-13: 978-0-373-64401-8

Special thanks and acknowledgment to
Travis Morgan for his contribution to this work.

JUNGLE HUNT

Do not call the forest that shelters you a jungle.
                    —African proverb

I often find that those who rape and pillage villages within
Third World nations think no one will notice or care. And I
am happy to show the perpetrators the error of their ways.
                    —Mack Bolan

# THE
# MACK BOLAN
## LEGEND

Nothing less than a war could have fashioned the destiny of the man called Mack Bolan. Bolan earned the Executioner title in the jungle hell of Vietnam.

But this soldier also wore another name—Sergeant Mercy. He was so tagged because of the compassion he showed to wounded comrades-in-arms and Vietnamese civilians.

Mack Bolan's second tour of duty ended prematurely when he was given emergency leave to return home and bury his family, victims of the Mob. Then he declared a one-man war against the Mafia.

He confronted the Families head-on from coast to coast, and soon a hope of victory began to appear. But Bolan had broken society's every rule. That same society started gunning for this elusive warrior—to no avail.

So Bolan was offered amnesty to work within the system against terrorism. This time, as an employee of Uncle Sam, Bolan became Colonel John Phoenix. With a command center at Stony Man Farm in Virginia, he and his new allies—Able Team and Phoenix Force—waged relentless war on a new adversary: the KGB.

But when his one true love, April Rose, died at the hands of the Soviet terror machine, Bolan severed all ties with Establishment authority.

Now, after a lengthy lone-wolf struggle and much soul-searching, the Executioner has agreed to enter an "arm's-length" alliance with his government once more, reserving the right to pursue personal missions in his Everlasting War.

# Prologue

*Quito, Ecuador*

The air in the large office, located in a nondescript building on a side street of the capital city, was humid and still, barely stirred by a slow-moving ceiling fan. The daily rain had already come, leaving a damp scent of water ignored by the two men in the room.

Jaime Cordero sat in the guest seat, a leather-upholstered wingback chair that squeaked with his every movement. A thin, stooped man, his shoulders were hunched from decades of civil service, service that had worn on him over the years, lined his face, eroded his stature, receded his hairline. His brown, off-the-rack suit hung on him like a scarecrow's costume, a stained tie loosely knotted around his neck. His watery brown eyes, magnified behind thick-lensed glasses, roamed nervously around the room, but always came back to rest on the alligator briefcase resting on top of the large mahogany desk.

The man sitting behind the desk was the exact opposite of Cordero in every way. Alfredo Roldos was the picture of health, his slightly protruding stomach hardly showing under the vest of his tailored navy three-piece Savile Row suit. His thick black hair, accented with just a touch of silver at his temples, was brushed back from a handsome widow's peak. His manicured hands were swift and sure as they clipped the end off a Don Conti Robusto. "Are you sure you won't join me?"

"N-no, Mr. Roldos—I simply wish to take care of our business."

"Of course, but I hope you do not mind if I indulge." Roldos applied an even blue flame from his butane lighter to the end of the cigar, drawing smoke slowly and letting it leak out the side of his mouth.

"No, sir."

Roldos savored his Robusto for another minute, exhaling the smoke in lazy plumes that were barely stirred by the overhead fan. Across the desk, leather squeaked as the other man shifted uneasily.

At length, Roldos set his cigar down in a mirror-bright silver ashtray. "Well, I suppose we should get down to business."

GALO MOVED SILENTLY through the sweltering tropical jungle, his bare feet making no noise on the thick carpet of rotting vegetation and wood. His breechclout covered his private parts, but the rest of his body was naked, decorated with bright red paint and a handwoven braided necklace. His curious brown eyes looked out at the world from a round face topped by straight black hair cut bowl-style. His unblinking gaze was currently fixed on the prize he sought a few yards away. Although the forest around him teemed with noisy insects and small animals, Galo tried his hardest not to make a sound as he crept forward.

The bird he was stalking, a toucan with primarily black feathers, save for an orange-and-red chest, with a red circle around its eye, shuffled along a branch, eyeing a cluster of guarana berries. Galo was only three yards away, then only two....

The rumble of a large engine in the distance silenced all of the nearby fauna and made Galo's head whip around. The red-breasted toucan he'd been stalking spread its wings and launched into the air.

A frown crossing his normally happy features, Galo took off through the jungle, leaping fallen tree trunks and avoiding dangling vines as he ran toward the source of the noise. It seemed to be coming closer to him, and he thought the vehicle must have been taking the single-lane road to his village.

Galo's heart quickened at the thought of visitors, who often brought strange and magical devices from the world outside their small jungle home. Small boxes that showed amazing pictures, devices that fit into a hand that allowed the holder to talk to someone they could not see, who might be a dozen, or even a hundred miles away. Perhaps he could even trade some of his wood carvings for a pair of the dark glasses that fit over his eyes and blocked the sun, or even, if he was lucky, a knife with a blade that folded into the handle like the one his father owned.

The tenor of the engine changed and Galo sensed the truck had stopped somewhere nearby. He crept through the thick foliage, mindful of the brightly colored tree frogs whose skin exuded a deadly poison, until he could see the olive-drab truck. When he did, his brows knitted in a frown—these were not the usual missionaries or traders that came to their isolated village. This truck looked menacing, a large interloper in the verdant, peaceful jungle.

And the men it carried—with their pale white skin and hair on their faces—were dressed in black clothes. But as he watched, they changed into long-sleeved shirts and pants that mimicked the greenery and shadows of his home. They didn't carry the usual equipment of those coming to trade with his village, either—each man had either in his hands or slung over his shoulder a big, long, black piece of metal that resembled the rifle his father used for hunting, but much uglier and more dangerous-looking. The men talked in a strange language and smoked cigarettes, the acrid smell making Galo's nose twitch and his mouth dry.

Another man dressed in tan clothes and a safari hat got out of the front of the truck and talked to the men in back

in their peculiar language. The smoking men all laughed as
they checked their large black rifles, then the leader walked
back to the front of the vehicle and got in, as the others
climbed into the back. The truck started moving again, heading toward Galo's village. He followed, paralleling the truck
through the jungle.

ROLDOS EXAMINED THE sheaf of papers the other man had
placed on his desk. He already knew what they contained, but
skimmed the odd paragraph here and there to ensure nothing
had been inserted at the last minute. "Everything seems to be
in order…mineral and logging rights for an area in Ecuador's
interior rainforest…" He named the longitude and latitude
coordinates. "And you're sure this is on the edge of Yasuní?"

Cordero nodded, his head bobbing on his neck like a stork.
"I checked the numbers myself—the territory abuts the park,
but does not encroach on it."

"Excellent. The ten-year term is listed here…" Although
I'm sure we won't need the space for nearly that long, Roldos
thought. "There is nothing left to do but sign." Taking a gold
Mont Blanc pen from his shirt pocket, Roldos signed the
copies where necessary with a bold flourish, then pushed the
assignation of rights contract back to Cordero, who hesitated
only slightly as he picked up the pen, his expression twisting on his strained face, as if suffering a late attack of con-
science.

Without saying a word, Roldos reached down for the
handle of the aluminum briefcase sitting on the floor behind
his desk, lifted it and set it on the table. Cordero's eyes widened when they fell upon the case.

"You—you promise that the indigenous peoples of the
area will not be harmed, *sim?*" he asked, his gaze lingering
on the case's smooth surface.

Roldos smiled, a warm, relaxed smile that lit up his face—
and stopped a mile short of reaching his eyes. "Jaime—
please. The natives are a huge part of our operation. We'll
need experienced guides who can show us the area and ex-

pedite access to the more remote regions. Making contact with them is crucial. We'll be compensating them well for the trouble," he lied.

The other man's head nodded almost unconsciously at Roldos's smooth voice. He bent over the contracts and scribbled his name on the line, sealing the deal.

When the last copy had been executed, three copies safely tucked away in Cordero's battered briefcase, with another set residing in the top drawer of Roldos's desk, he slid the metal case across the desktop toward the other man. With slightly trembling fingers, Cordero reached for the case, almost clutching it to his chest before restraining himself and setting it on his lap. His head came up as he looked at his benefactor, the naked question all over his face.

Roldos permitted himself a slight chuckle and waved his hand. "It's all right, my friend. You will not insult me—if I were in your shoes, I would want to look inside, too. Go ahead, you've earned it."

Cordero flipped the catches on the case and slowly opened it, inhaling audibly when he saw what was inside—two hundred and fifty thousand U.S. dollars, enough for him and his family to live comfortably for the rest of their lives.

"Thank you, Alfredo, thank you." Cordero closed the case again, stood and shook Roldos's hand.

"No, my friend, thank you." Roldos escorted the Assistant Secretary of the Interior to the door, said goodbye and made sure his secretary showed him the way out.

Once he was alone, he closed the door and locked it. Striding back to his desk, he sat and took a satellite phone from another desk drawer. Activating it, he dialed a number from memory. It rang three times, then a connection was made.

*"Ja?"*

"The contract is signed. Begin the operation."

*"Ja."*

Roldos broke the connection, put the phone away and reached for his Robusto again, intending to smoke it down to the butt. *And in a few days, we'll be on our way to making more money than anyone's ever seen.*

STILL TRAILING THE TRUCK, Galo scrambled across a large tree trunk that had fallen the day before and presently spanned a plant-choked ravine. The voracious denizens of the rainforest were already going to work on it, however, and soon it would be eaten away and fall into the divide, to rot and return to the earth. But for the moment, it made an excellent natural bridge.

On the other side, Galo scurried through the underbrush, with less than fifty yards to go until he reached the village clearing. He was about to emerge from the jungle and greet the visitors when he heard screams, followed by a sound he knew all too well—the sharp crack of gunfire.

Dropping to his stomach, Galo crawled forward until he was able to peek under a large cluster of purple orchids and watch what was happening to his friends and family.

The men from the truck, their heads covered by cloth masks, were all out of the vehicle and splitting up throughout the village, which consisted of about a dozen thin-walled huts on stilts with thatched roofs. The inhabitants, including Galo's mother and father, had been coming out to greet the newcomers, but presently ran in terror, only managing a few steps before being gunned down and dropping in their tracks. The men were focused, efficient and deadly. Two-man teams moved from hut to hut, checking inside and shooting anyone they found. Screams of terror were cut off instantly by bursts of automatic-rifle fire.

Galo was frozen where he lay, mouth locked open in a silent scream, unable to run, unable to move. In a few minutes it was all over, save for the occasional single shot as the merciless killers swept through the village one last time, finishing off the wounded. A burst of rifle fire sounded in the distance, and a pair of the camouflaged men emerged from the jungle on the far end of the village, their rifles smoking as they laughed to each other.

The man in the cab, the leader of the operation, stood on the running board of the large truck, face partially shaded by the safari hat, his light blue eyes sweeping across the shattered remains of the village and the motionless bodies of its inhabitants.

The men regrouped at the truck, climbing in only when the man in the hat gave the signal. The vehicle turned around in the clearing and had begun heading out when it came to a halt. The man in the hat rolled his window down and peered out at the jungle—right where Galo was hiding.

Ducking his head, the boy held his breath, not daring to move. The truck stayed where it was for what seemed like an eternity. Galo's heart hammered in his chest as he expected to hear the savage bark of the killers' rifles any second. He was steeling himself to jump up and run deeper into the forest when the truck's engine revved up again and it moved out down the road, its growl growing fainter and fainter until he could no longer hear it.

Yet still Galo stayed where he lay, under the orchids, not daring to move.

A light rain began falling on Galo, the slaughtered village…everything.

Still, the boy did not move.

# 1

Even dressed in khaki chinos and a bright tropical shirt—dark blue with palm trees and red-and-yellow macaws patterned all over it—Mack Bolan felt underdressed as he moved through the huge, raucous dance party in the *favela* of Rocinha, one of Rio de Janeiro's worst slums. Even the police feared coming into the seemingly endless blocks of closely packed, brightly colored two- and three-story tenements, each of which often contained several families living almost on top of each other.

Rio's government, however, was prepping for the 2016 Olympics, and high priority was to clean up the *favelas* and crack down on the flourishing crime spawned there, especially the drug trade.

That was why Bolan was here. Street intelligence said that Thiago Bernier, one of the city's top drug lords, was making a rare public appearance here, accepting tribute from the slum dwellers while presiding as the unofficial "king" of the *baile,* or dance party. Although Stony Man and the U.S. government typically left internal policing to the respective country, Bernier was the middleman in a smuggling ring that stretched across South America, from the Atlantic to the Pacific and all the way up to Mexico. When the local police were less than forthcoming about providing intelligence and assistance on his operation, Bolan had decided to handle things his way: get into the country, find Bernier and bring him out—one way or another. The resistance had been just enough for Bolan to consider whether officers inside the department had been bribed by the ever-present tide of drug money washing over the city, but that investigation would have to wait for another time.

Typically, Anglos stood out anywhere they went in the sprawling metropolis. Besides his clothes, Bolan had disguised himself with a spray-on tan. With his black hair, he figured he'd blend in well enough, even if he was several inches taller than the majority of the dancing, singing, drinking crowd around him.

Fortunately, even his loud shirt was positively subdued compared to the riot of color and sound surrounding him. Remixed bossa nova music blared from speakers on every block, the pulsating beat driving men and women, all dressed in bright costumes, to dance wildly all around him. Bolan could even understand the frenetic activity—celebrate life this day, because any one of the partygoers around him could be dead tomorrow. It wasn't a philosophy he subscribed to—whenever possible, he preferred to be the one holding the gun.

Although he tried to stick close to the sides of buildings, occasionally knots of partiers would sweep him into the maelstrom that was the nonstop street party. So far, besides spotting several hired guns positioned throughout the revelers, Bolan hadn't seen a concentrated force yet—he figured that was coming soon, and he was right.

A vacant lot had been taken over to install Bernier as the king of festivities. Swarthy, black-haired and handsome, he presided over the party with a casual bored air of the slumming kingpin. One thing Bolan had to give him credit for was the number of pigs roasting in pits around the lot. The rich smell of the roasting pork overlaid the strong smell of cheap cologne, sweat and filth that permeated the street. At least the attendees'll eat well this night, Bolan thought. Assuming they survive the next few minutes.

A flash of movement across the street attracted his predator senses and Bolan glanced over to see a brief altercation already being broken up by several people. It was enough, however, for him to spot a familiar-looking face, topped by a shock of black hair with a distinctive streak of white.

*Davi Giachetto*—the police are here? Although annoyed, Bolan wasn't surprised that his own source had made sure the local brass had shown up. He got paid twice, and there was a better-than-even chance that one or both of the parties using the information would be killed in the ensuing firefight, leaving him in the clear. It was actually pretty clever. Bolan made a mental note to himself that if he ever saw that snitch again, he'd be sure to remind him how much he didn't like being sold out.

But that was then—now, he had to prevent a potential bloodbath. Bolan had nothing against the short, tireless Brazilian cop. Sergeant Giachetto had cojones the size of soccer balls to even come down here in the first place. He had to know that if he was made, he'd be dead before he got to the end of the block.

But just because Bolan liked the man didn't mean he trusted him. After all, what better way to eliminate a competitor in crime than to bribe a cop to arrest the man, then have him shot while "resisting arrest" or "attempting to escape." Although he was usually on the side of the badges, Bolan had run into his share of bent police officers in the past and always approached every one he met with the same amount of caution and skepticism until he was sure of their loyalty.

Raising his smartphone, he took a picture of the street's festivities, making sure to catch the officer in the shot. As he did, Bolan ran another casual sweep of the narrow avenue, revising his assessment of the posted security. Even as he watched, three of them had already been neutralized and replaced with Giachetto's men. Slick, he thought, pushing his way to the front of the empty lot, which was guarded by three men several inches taller than him and twice as wide.

*"Eu tenho que ver o Senhor Bernier,"* Bolan said in passable Portuguese. His smartphone's translator program was

just hitting beta test in the U.S. Army. Bolan was part of the field testing, right here, right now.

*"Ninguém vê o Senhor Bernier,"* one of the big men grunted, shaking his head. "No one sees Mr. Bernier."

*"É urgente. Eu trabalho para o Alarico Nascimento."* Bolan cautiously pulled up his shirt to reveal his smartphone in a holster at his waist, noting the man's large hand creeping behind his back. The bodyguard on Bolan's left was backing up his partner while the third man kept watch over the boisterous crowd. These guys were definitely not local muscle for hire—they were professionals.

When the bodyguard saw the phone, he nodded his massive head once. Bolan speed-dialed a number and handed the phone to the hulk. *"Leve isso para o Senhor Bernier."*

The big man stared at Bolan for a moment, looked suspiciously at the phone, dwarfed in his huge paw, then turned and lumbered into the lot, the two other guards closing ranks behind him. He reached Bernier, who was watching a pair of scantily clad women dance in front of him while texting on his own smartphone.

The kingpin looked up at his henchman over his round glasses, then followed the other man's finger as it pointed out Bolan. Frowning, he took the phone and put it to his ear. Bolan watched Bernier stiffen as he heard his lieutenant, Alarico Nascimento, tell him that the bearer of this phone should be trusted implicitly, as he had been sent by Nascimento himself to Bernier. The drug dealer stared at Bolan again, then spoke to his guard and pointed at Bolan, who casually rested his hand on his hip—the better to draw his compact SIG Sauer pistol hidden at the small of his back if needed.

The big man whispered in his cohort's ear, then waved Bolan forward. He slipped past the two men, taking the opportunity to look behind him for any sign of the *polícia*. He thought he caught a glimpse of Giachetto's face in the crowd, but an exuberant dancer crossed in front of him, cutting off his view. Then Bolan was behind the bodyguard wall, walking to Bernier's cheap wooden throne.

"You work for Alarico?" the dealer asked in Portuguese.

"Yes," Bolan answered.

"Why are you here?" Bernier asked.

"He sent me to warn you—the police are coming, tonight, for you, right now." All of that was true—Nascimento had been captured by Stony Man operatives while on vacation in Canada and had provided Bolan's bona fides as part of a witness protection deal.

Bernier slouched back in his chair and laughed. "The fucking police wouldn't dare show their faces in the *favelas!*"

Bolan held his hand out for his smartphone, which Bernier tossed at him with a sneer. Flicking through the screens, Bolan brought up the photograph he'd taken of the street a few minutes ago and zoomed in on Giachetto's face. Holding the phone out, he asked, "You recognize this cop?"

Bernier stiffened when he saw the sergeant's face. "Shit! That son of a bitch!" He whistled, a sharp blast that brought his bodyguard back. Bernier hissed commands that made the man get on his cell, most likely trying to raise the other security guards in the area. Bolan looked at the front of the lot to see the other men not even bothering to hide their weapons, each one carrying a compact Steyr Tactical Machine Pistol with extended magazine. Bolan kept his expression carefully neutral at the sight, although he realized that the possibility of a slaughter had just increased by a factor of ten. The Steyrs were compact "room brooms," spitting out 9 mm bullets at 850 rounds per minute. If the police mishandled the arrest, the resulting riot could leave dozens injured or dead.

Bernier sprang from his chair. "Javiero! Let's get the fuck outta here! You—" he pointed at Bolan "—you're coming with us, as well. If this is a double cross, you'll be the first to die! Get moving!"

Keeping his hands in plain sight, Bolan walked ahead of Javiero the bodyguard. They were heading toward the back of the lot and a sleek Range Rover with tinted windows when a flurry of gunshots cracked from the crowd.

"Shit!" Bolan spun to hear the staccato bursts of the Steyrs as they spat death into the crowd. Screams and shouts ensued as the panicked men and woman tried to scatter for cover, running into each other and trampling several in their haste to escape the kill zone.

"Javiero! Cover me!" Bernier had drawn his own pistol, a chrome-plated Desert Eagle, and was covering Bolan with it. "You're my insurance."

"Whatever you say—but I wouldn't go out the back—" was all Bolan got to say before Bernier shoved the pistol under his chin.

"Why? You trying to lead me into a trap so *os porcos* can arrest me?"

"No, but the police'll have that covered, as well."

Just then another fusillade of shots sounded from ahead of them, and Bernier's driver exchanged fire with unseen assailants before driving off in a squeal of tires.

"Bastard! *Aquele cachorro!*" Bernier swore as Javiero let loose with his machine pistol, the roar of the compact weapon drowning out the rest of the man's swearing. He kept the cops under cover while moving to fire from behind the only protection he could find—one of the roasting pigs. Bullets punched through the carcass, spraying juices through the air.

Several cartridges also tunneled through the meat and into the huge bodyguard, making him sit with a surprised look on his face, his machine pistol slipping from his hand as he died.

**2**

*"Merda!* Now what?" Bernier stared at his dead guard in shock.

"This way!" Bolan shoved the Desert Eagle out of the way and yanked the kingpin toward the light green building on their left, which had every window and door boarded up. "Gimme that!" Snatching the large-caliber pistol out of the other man's hand, he aimed it at a covered window and fired four rounds, blowing one of the wooden slats in two. Yanking the broken pieces away, Bolan was about to enlarge the hole when a machete blade chunked down on the windowsill from inside. Bolan aimed high and fired two more rounds through the wood, making the blade vanish along with pounding feet as the people inside fled from the gunfire.

Bullets cracked into the mortar wall around them. Bolan pointed the Eagle backward, still angling the barrel up, and emptied the magazine, making everyone in the vicinity duck for cover. "Get inside!" he shouted at Bernier as he smashed out more planks with the butt of the pistol.

Bernier scrambled through the narrow gap, with Bolan right behind him. The room they found themselves in was dark and small, yet still contained a cube refrigerator, table and shelves against one wall. A doorway opened into more blackness. The room stank of thousands of old meals, sweat and despair.

Grabbing his charge by the sleeve, Bolan shoved him

against the wall next to the door. "Got any spare mags for this?"

Bernier nodded, handing over two 9-round magazines. Bolan reloaded the large pistol, then drew his own SIG Sauer, readying both as his eyes adjusted to the gloom. Outside, the gunfire continued, with the police apparently pinned down. Bolan grimaced at the thought—they might need the military to come get them, but if that was the case, they'd probably be dead before help arrived.

"Shouldn't I get my gun back?" Bernier pouted.

"Not if you wanna get out of here alive," Bolan said. "Now be quiet." He listened to the noises inside the building—scurrying feet, hushed whispers. "If these people recognize your voice, tell them you'll reward them in exchange for assistance out of here."

Bernier stepped forward and called into the hallway, rattling off several sentences in rapid Portuguese. There was another conference, then a slight form emerged out of the darkness—a girl about fourteen years old.

"Come here, child." Bernier waved her forward. "You take myself and my friend out of here safely, and I will reward you and your family handsomely."

Shaking her head, she held out a grimy hand.

Bernier chuckled. "They learn young," he said as he pulled out an alligator-skin wallet.

"Yeah, well, she's gonna learn what a bullet in the face feels like if we don't get out of here quick."

Bernier held out a hundred dollar bill, but when the girl moved to grab it, neatly tore it in two. "This half and two more when we are safely away."

The girl stared at him, then nodded as she turned and began walking down the corridor. Bernier exchanged a glance with Bolan, who nodded. "She's our ticket out."

The kingpin started walking down the dark hallway, with Bolan bringing up the rear, one pistol pointed ahead, the other behind him. Doorways—empty frames and also holes cut into the walls, some covered with hanging blankets, others empty and gaping—lined the hallway on both sides.

Bolan wasn't claustrophobic, but the narrow passage plus the lack of light and multiple attack vectors were sending his senses into overdrive. He was crazily alert to every noise in the place, and there were many—too many. The only good news was that they seemed to be leaving any pursuit behind.

The girl led them up a cramped staircase, the steps concave, worn from years of feet tramping up and down. Bolan caught the aroma of wood smoke and vegetables sizzling—someone was cooking nearby. The stairs opened into another hallway, identical to the first one, with rooms on either side. Bolan tried to watch every direction as they went down it, but he had to trust that the girl was really taking them out—a dangerous proposition here, where both Bernier and he could disappear, their bodies never to be found again.

Shouts and crashes echoed up the stairwell, making Bolan quicken his pace. The girl ducked under a tattered blanket into a room at the end of the hall, waving them forward. Bernier hurried to follow.

"Wait—!" Bolan's whispered warning came too late. He tucked the SIG away and, leading with the Desert Eagle, pushed into the room—only to feel a circle of cold steel press into his neck. Bolan froze, the Desert Eagle held with its muzzle pointing in the air as he took in the room. A frown on her face, the girl stood by a crude rope ladder leading to a trapdoor in the ceiling. Two other men besides the punk holding the gun on Bolan stood in the room. One had a pistol trained on Bernier, the other held an iron pipe, ready to reinforce either of his criminal partners.

"Drop the pist—" was all the gunman had time to say before Bolan snaked his arm around the shooter's wrist, levering the gun out of line on him and trapping it between his elbow and side. The moment the pistol was neutralized, he leveled the Desert Eagle and put a round into the second gunman's chest, the boom of the .357 deafening in the small room.

Steadying the guy with his left hand, Bolan pulled him close as he brought his forehead down, smashing it into the thug's nose. Cartilage crunched and blood squirted as the guy screamed in agony. Releasing him, Bolan stripped the pistol from his hand as he fell to the floor, keeping it locked between his arm and his side.

In the three seconds it had taken to do that, the pipe-wielding man charged at Bolan, wildly swinging his pipe. Trying to aim the Desert Eagle at his attacker, the end of the pipe connected with the large gun's frame hard enough to jar it out of Bolan's hand. The shiny pistol skittered across the floor, but Bolan couldn't track it, as all his attention was on the man in front of him, who was already cocking the pipe for another swing. There was no time to draw the SIG again, so Bolan went for the pistol under his arm. Pulling it out, he cocked the hammer back on the revolver and snap-fired as soon as he had it out far enough to line up the stubby barrel on the guy's face. As he squeezed the trigger, Bolan felt tape on the handle and hoped the Saturday Night Special didn't blow up in his hand.

It did something far worse—the hammer fell on a chamber, but no bullet fired. It was a dud.

"Hell!" Bolan ducked underneath the man's wild swing, the pipe coming close enough to him to ruffle his hair. He was about to step forward and hammer the pistol butt into the man's face when the left side of his head simply exploded, demolishing his facial features, as well. At the same time, another thunderous boom reverberated in the room, painfully hammering Bolan's eardrums. The man's body followed his brains, toppling over on his side to the floor.

He glanced over to see Bernier aiming the smoking Desert Eagle at the girl, who just stood and stared back at him. He nodded at the three dead men, the question obvious. Shaking her head, she spit on the nearest one, then pointed up at the trapdoor again.

Bolan watched this all with his eardrums feeling as though they were stuffed full of cotton. Dimly he heard noise from outside, in the hallway. Bernier heard it, as well, for he walked to the doorway, stuck the pistol out and fired three rounds. Pointing it at the girl, he waved her up the ladder. She scrambled up like a monkey, pushing the trapdoor—just a piece of plywood, no doubt scavenged from a construction site—out of the way and climbing out onto the roof.

"Go!" SIG Sauer in hand, Bolan covered the doorway, first kicking the guy with the broken nose in the head to ensure he couldn't tell anyone where they had gone. Bernier hoisted himself up the rope ladder. Only when he was outside did Bolan holster his gun and shimmy up. The moment he was on the roof, he grabbed the rope and pulled it up after him, then shoved the plywood back into place.

The rooftop they were on was indistinguishable from a thousand others around them. Gunshots still sounded from the street below, but they'd become more sporadic. Bernier and Bolan looked around for the best way out.

"You have a car somewhere, right?" the kingpin asked.

Bolan pointed. "Yeah, six blocks that way—if it hasn't been stolen or stripped yet. We should try to find other wheels anyway. The police will be looking for newer vehicles coming out of here."

Bernier turned to the girl and asked her a question. In response, she held out her hand. "Damn it!" He counted off four more hundred-dollar bills, plus the torn half of the first one. "Let's go!"

The girl scurried off, leading the two men to the back wall, where a plank she placed between two buildings served as an improvised bridge. Although it creaked under Bolan's two hundred pounds, it held him as he crossed.

They went across three more rooftops, ascending the stacked buildings of the *favela* until coming to a single-lane road. The girl trotted past three houses until she came to what looked like a crude garage with a door made of jury-rigged corrugated tin sheets, secured with a brand-new, shiny padlock. The girl pointed to it, then held out her hand a third time.

"Gonna be broke by the time we leave," Bernier grumbled, but counted another five hundred dollars into her hand. "Go, get out of here, you extortionist." The girl made the last payment disappear as quickly as she had the first one, then whirled and dashed off down an alley, gone from sight in seconds.

"How are we getting in?" Bernier asked, pointing the pistol at the lock.

"No! Shooting's too loud—it'll draw everyone to us. Just keep watch." Bolan bent down and got to work with his picks. Two minutes later, the lock was picked. Pulling the door open revealed a battered Subaru Brat, minus the hood and with dented and rusty doors and side panels. "Haven't seen one of these in forever. Let's go."

"Can you get it started?" Bernier asked as he got in on the passenger side.

"Of course." Bolan exposed the steering column of the almost thirty-year-old vehicle, stripped the right wires and touched them together. The light truck's engine sputtered and coughed. Bolan pumped the gas once and touched the wires together again. This time the Subaru turned over with an ear-splitting racket—apparently the muffler was long gone, too.

"Let's go!" Bernier shouted. "I got a feeling this wasn't hers to sell!"

"You and me both!" Bolan pressed the brake, then engaged the clutch and gave it gas. The little two-seater shook its way out of the garage just as two men came around the corner, one carrying an ax handle, the other clutching an old, double-barreled shotgun. When they saw their vehicle being stolen, the shotgunner aimed his weapon.

"Down!" Bernier shouted as the back window disintegrated in a shower of glass pellets behind them. Bolan cranked the wheel hard right and hit the gas, making the Subaru leap ahead as it lurched into gear. Bernier stuck his Desert Eagle out the passenger window and cranked off the rest of his magazine, making the two men duck for cover.

Downshifting into second, Bolan made the Subaru fly

down the single lane, praying no one stepped out into the road, as he wouldn't be able to stop and there was nowhere to swerve. The alley remained empty, fortunately, and he took the first road they came to, cranking left to get back onto one of the main roads and out of the slum.

"Incredible! You are something else!" Bernier had put away his pistol and stared at Bolan in admiration. "A man of your talents shouldn't be wasted on Alarico. How about you come work for me? At triple your previous pay, of course!"

"That is a very generous offer, Senhor Bernier. Let's get out of the city first, and then we can discuss my new arrangements—and my payment."

"Of course, of course." Bernier took out his smartphone. "I can have my jet ready to go in an hour. Head to Galeão."

Bolan kept his smile to himself—the international airport twenty minutes away from the city was where they were headed anyway.

They negotiated the afternoon traffic to get on the highway and were soon cruising along underneath the bright sun, the carnage of a half hour ago rapidly receding. Bernier smoked a cheroot and talked expansively, promising Bolan a top position in his cartel. "Maybe even to replace that weasel Alarico—his payments have been a little light recently. I think you could handle his operations very nicely."

For his part, Bolan kept his eyes on the road and nodded where appropriate.

"The Gulfstream is in hangar 11E, just head right down, they're expecting us."

Bolan took the turnoff to the private hangars, but as 11E came up, he didn't turn toward it.

Bernier looked at his jet as they drove past his hangar. "What are you doing? It's back there, you missed it…" He trailed off when he saw the SIG Sauer in Bolan's hand pointed at him.

"I'm afraid I came to you under false pretenses, Senhor Bernier. I'm not going with you—you're coming with me.

What condition you're in during the flight, however, is completely up to you."

Bernier's gaze rose to his face, and Bolan knew exactly what he was thinking. Could he draw and shoot before he fired? Bolan shook his head slowly. "I wouldn't." Bernier slumped back in his seat.

They turned into another hangar, where a larger Gulfstream jet was idling on the tarmac. A tall man with light brown hair and dressed in a summer-weight tropical sport coat, open-collared shirt and sunglasses stood by the open stairway. Bolan pulled to a stop in front of him.

"Afternoon, Mack." The man's voice had a thick layer of cockney in it.

"David."

"Any problems?"

"Nothing I couldn't handle."

The head of Phoenix Force shook his head. "Still say it would have been more prudent to have me with you."

Bolan smiled. "I wanted to get one man out, David, not bring down the entire slum around me."

"Fair enough." David McCarter moved to the passenger door. "This our third passenger?"

"Yup."

McCarter grinned, a sharklike baring of teeth that was completely devoid of warmth or humor. "You aren't gonna be any trouble now, are you, mate?"

Staring at the fox-faced Brit, Bernier shook his head. David reached in and relieved him of his sidearm and smartphone. "All right, then, time to go."

It was on the way to the plane that Bernier got some of his courage back. "Wait a minute. You cannot just take me out of the country—there are rules to this sort of thing. I cannot be extradited like this. I demand to speak to your State Depart..." He trailed off at seeing the wolfish looks on Bolan's and David's faces.

"When are these guys gonna learn?" David asked rhetorically.

"I never claimed to be affiliated with the government, U.S. or otherwise."

Bernier's face clouded in confusion. "What—are you bounty hunters? Private security? Whatever you're being paid, I can give you ten times the amount."

David dropped a firm, unyielding hand on the Brazilian drug lord's shoulder. "You can just call us troubleshooters, mate. And if you're not nice and polite on the flight up, you'll be the trouble we'll shoot next."

Thiago Bernier, once a top drug kingpin and mastermind behind a large pipeline that stretched from Rio to Peru and three other continents, allowed himself to be meekly led into the Gulfstream's interior, searched in more detail and secured to a captain's chair.

Meanwhile, Bolan contacted their pilot, Jack Grimaldi, and had him get into the takeoff schedule. Thirty minutes later, they were wheels up and off the ground, arrowing into the brilliant blue Brazilian sky.

**3**

Once Bernier had been settled—with the aid of a mild sedative to relax him—Bolan had planned to take a well-deserved break himself, having been up for the past thirty hours tracking down his leads to the drug lord. McCarter, however, had other plans for him.

"Sorry, mate, but Hal said to call in the moment you got here." He dropped his rangy form into the cushy leather seat across from Bolan. "You're lucky I let you have a drink first."

"Well, I already noticed we're not heading north." Bolan gestured with his bottle of water at the sun setting ahead of them. "What's he got now?"

David shrugged as he held out a sat phone. "No idea—your ears only, apparently. All I know is that I get to babysit Mr. Silk Pants there back to D.C. while you get to jaunt off into the shite again."

Bolan grinned as he took the receiver. "Too bad there couldn't be another mission in Rio—preferably on the beach?"

"Oi, mate, wild horses wouldn't have kept me from *that* one." McCarter rose. "I'm gonna go check on our passenger."

"Thanks." Bolan waited until David had headed out before connecting to Stony Man Farm, his stateside base of operations. Bounced off several satellites, the tight-beam communication went through multiple encryption layers, rendering it virtually unbreakable. To the rest of the world, Bolan and his contact outside of Washington, D.C., were speaking static-filled gibberish.

"Striker?" Bolan heard a quiet chewing sound and knew Brognola was munching on one of his ever-present antacid tablets.

"I'm here, Hal."

"How was your fishing trip?"

Bolan grinned. "Not as much time on the beach as I'd wanted, but I landed the big one. David cleaned him up and we're bringing him home so you can cook him for as long as you want."

"Excellent. Look, normally I don't like sending you back out in the field right after the completion of one mission, however, Wonderland's breathing down my neck on this one, and since you're already in the area, so to speak..."

"Yeah, it seems I can't get enough of South America lately. Where's Jack dropping me off this time?"

"Quito, Ecuador, and from there you'll be taking a charter plane to Neuva Loja, in the province of Sucumbíos. Ultimately you'll be heading into the Amazon rainforest, so let me know whatever gear you'll need that isn't on the plane and we'll drop it to you."

"Okay—what's going on over there?"

"Part of this—okay, most of this—is the D.C. policy wonks and bureaucrats covering their collective asses. As I'm sure you're aware, the energy crisis is ramping up again, with oil futures climbing to record levels again and showing no signs of receding anytime soon. With truly effective alternate power sources still slow to come online, efficient use of current fields and discovery of new ones is of paramount importance, not only to our current government, but also to nations around the world."

No surprise there, Bolan thought. China's appetite for energy grew larger by the week, with India nipping at its neighbor's heels, both burgeoning nations contributing to the pall of pollution growing worse in the Far East every day. And that didn't even count America's near-insatiable consumption of gasoline—all of which required new sources, preferably not from the Middle East.

"Of course, this has pushed any and all forms of oil exploration to the forefront, with companies able to find and claim the biggest undiscovered fields reaping potential years, maybe even decades of bonanza. Recent explorations indicate sizable oil fields are present in several areas of the Amazonian rainforest, particularly on the border between Ecuador and Colombia. The oil exploration company Sulexco has recently entered into an agreement to measure exactly how much oil may be in the area."

"I trust that you're not asking our operatives to babysit oil company executives?" Bolan kept his tone even, but his disdain was evident at the thought of such an assignment.

Brognola snorted. "Hell, no. They've hired a private security company to provide corporate protection for its assets. However, despite the U.S. and Ecuador's warm camaraderie in public, they've been making some moves lately that the current administration is not very happy with, including getting very cozy with Iran over the past couple of years."

Bolan sifted through recent CIA analysis on his smartphone. "Yeah, they've been buying weapons from the Middle East, taking billions in deposits, everything but a government sleepover. But why send me to the middle of nowhere? If there's something to be found, shouldn't I be starting in the capital?"

"Normally, yes, but the Ecuador-Colombian border is important for a couple other reasons. Although the two countries have recently put an end to their hostilities, things tensed up again in '08 after a Colombian military action against FARC rebels left twenty dead, and relations between the two countries strained to the breaking point. And I haven't even mentioned how chummy Ecuador's president is with Venezuela yet—and we know what Chavez thinks of America. The U.S. wants the oil folks to get their work done smoothly and to ensure that no rogue elements on any side—FARC, the Colombian military, *anybody*—inflame any tensions that could spark a full-scale war. The idea is to send you down there to keep the peace and head off anything before it makes headlines."

"And I'm guessing that any intervention by American forces would be seen as the U.S. sticking its nose where it doesn't belong," Bolan said.

"Got it in one, Striker. With the Ecuadorian president still clinging to power after an attempted police coup in 2010, State doesn't want to do any on-the-record poking around down there unless we're sure folks're being naughty. That, of course, is where you come in."

"Of course. Do I have a cover, or am I just supposed to run around the jungle and see who shoots at me first?"

"We're inserting you using the Cooper alias—you've decided to head down and report on the state of the rainforest, find out the real story about oil drilling there, that sort of Pulitzer prize–grabbing material. Your modified jacket's already on the way and will be in place before you're on the ground. Once there, I'm sure you'll root out anything that's happening soon enough."

"Fair enough. Give me any updates on the locals from the Agency, and I'll review them on the way over. South America's been fun so far—I'm sure Ecuador will be, too."

"That's the spirit. With luck you'll just tour the countryside, and everything will be nice and peaceful."

"Hal, they wouldn't be sending me down there if that was the case—you know that."

"Hey, I can dream, can't I?" Brognola grumbled. "Just keep your powder and your feet dry, Striker. Call in when you touch down in Neuva Loja. We'll work out the rest from there."

"Will do. Striker out." He'd no sooner disconnected when McCarter stuck his head over the seat.

"Back into it, eh?"

"Yup, apparently there may be some unrest brewing west of here—White House wants it checked out."

"Lucky bastard—trade you details?" The Brit's tone was hopeful.

"No chance, David. The rainforest still needs to be standing once I'm done there."

"Hey, I'd leave most of it intact." McCarter actually sounded wounded by Bolan's gibe.

"Still, they asked for me and that's what they're gonna get. I'm sure something'll come up that needs your unique talents soon enough." Bolan reclined his seat and closed the window shade. "I'm gonna catch a couple hours' sleep before running prep. Make sure our guest is comfortable and quiet."

"Can do." McCarter went back to check on Bernier again, while Bolan immediately dropped off.

SIXTEEN HOURS LATER, Bolan sat on a rickety bus as it brought him and a handful of other passengers from the only airport in Neuva Loja to the center of town. He'd been reading up on the capital of the province while on the flight over, learning that it was the central nexus for the various oil companies that had come in to prospect and drill.

Although the town had grown over the past several decades, the blight the oil companies had brought with them was plain to see. Acres and acres of fields were denuded and barren, deforested to make room for more buildings or the leavings of 20,000 people that were thrown away each day. The air carried with it that unique odor that came with oil drilling—a blend of burning fuel, hot metal and sweat that lingered in the back of the throat and on clothes and skin.

As they drove farther into town, Bolan was hard-pressed to find any difference between many of the city blocks they passed and the Rocinha slum. The buildings here were all packed tightly together, as well. The only difference being that they looked a little newer.

The bus dropped him off at the Hotel Araza, a neat, modern-looking three-story hotel with its own garage and security gate. Bolan walked in after a group of what looked like ecotourists. They ranged in age from college students to middle-aged men and women, wearing a variety of natural fibers, handwoven sandals and, at least for the men, a few scraggly beards.

He checked in under his Matt Cooper alias and went up to his room, which was spacious, with a tiled floor and free internet. Bolan swept it for bugs—more out of force of habit than anything else—then checked in with Stony Man Farm. With nothing new to report, he headed down for dinner.

As expected, he found several of the group on the bus sitting down to dinner, as well, all of them discussing the menu, which, of course, was printed in Portuguese. The three he pegged as college students were all snickering about the *caldo de manguera* soup, which they were trying to get the others to try. Bolan decided to play along and ordered it as his first course, following it with *llapingachos,* cheesy potato cakes served with grilled steak.

When his soup arrived, full of rice, celery and small chunks of meat swimming in a brown broth, Bolan didn't hesitate, but dug in, knowing full well that the other group was watching him to gauge his reaction.

Finally, one of them, a red-haired student in a woven native long-sleeved shirt and cargo shorts, pushed back his chair. "Dude, you do know what you're eating, right?"

Bolan nodded as he chewed, then swallowed one of the rubbery chunks of meat. "If my Portuguese is right, it's bull penis."

The other table erupted in various reactions, from laughter to disgust. "So, what's it taste like?" a shorter girl with her blond hair braided into two thick pigtails asked.

"Not like chicken, if that's what you're wondering. In fact, it doesn't really have much taste at all. Not like some of the other foods I've tasted. In fact, one of the worst was a delicacy called *balut,* that they serve in the Philippines." In between spoonfuls of soup, Bolan described the snack— basically a fertilized duck egg boiled whole and eaten straight out of the shell—with enough detail to make more than one of the group push their main course away with queasy looks on their faces.

After that, he was in. Bolan introduced himself as Matt Cooper and said he was a freelance reporter on assignment to do an in-depth report on the state of the Amazon rainforest. He barely got that out when one of the other students piped up.

"Dude, if you want a *real* story, you should totally come with us—we're heading into the deep jungle to volunteer at a Huaorani village." He introduced himself as Mike Saderson and said he and the others were part of the South American Relief Effort, or SARE. The next morning they were all heading to a remote village deep in the rainforest. "The indigenous tribesmen are being encroached upon by oil companies, not to mention illegal loggers, hunters and smugglers. SARE tries to improve their way of life and help protect them and the rainforest from depredation."

"Sounds like I might have just stumbled onto my story right here." Bolan's main course of *llapingachos* arrived, and as he dug in, he cast his gaze around at the rest of the group. "So, you're all here on the same mission?"

Each member at the table took a turn to introduce themselves, as Bolan sized them up. The group's makeup was about what he'd figured. The three college students—Saderson, Thomas Bonell and the shorter girl, Calley Carter—were looking for adventure while doing their part to save the world. The dark-haired man, Paul Wilberson, looked like a die-hard eco-nut or conservationist and turned out to be a little of each, along with possessing a degree in animal husbandry. The second woman was Susanna Tatrow, a British anthropologist graduate student who was going to be both studying and teaching at the tiny school in the village.

The last guy intrigued Bolan the most, primarily because he didn't fit into any easily classifiable niche. He was the last one to speak, and all he said was, "My name's Elliot Morgan, and I'm here because I wanted to see the ends of the earth." He glanced around. "Looks like I've come to the right place."

"You can say that again. Any of you ever been out in the deep rainforest before?" Shaking heads greeted Bolan's question. "It's quite an experience—I'd tell you more, but I don't want to color your first impressions. As long as you have all your shots up-to-date, you'll be fine.

"In fact," he said as he rose from the table, "I'd suggest you all get a good night's sleep—it's gonna be a long trip tomorrow."

"Are you going to join us out there, Matt?" Thomas Bonell asked.

"That's the plan, if SARE doesn't mind me tagging along. But right now, I've gotta check in with my bureau chief, make sure he doesn't have a problem with it. See you all in the morning."

He left the restaurant to a chorus of goodbyes, but waited until he'd reached his room before calling Stony Man Farm.

"Stony Man Farm, you kill 'em, we chill 'em," a young, familiar voice said on the other end.

"Akira, didn't Hal warn you about answering the sat line that way?" Bolan asked.

"Yeah, but what can I say—it just didn't take." Akira Tokaido was Stony Man's current computer expert, working with long-time stalwart Aaron "the Bear" Kurtzman. Among the youngest of the Stony Man team, his youth gave him a different way of looking at things—which sometimes worked against him. "What you need, Striker?"

"Dig up whatever you can find on a NGO called South American Relief Effort and send me any information on them. I've just been invited to join a group of volunteers heading out into the jungle and want to know what I'm getting into there."

"Gotcha, I'm on it." Bolan heard the clack of computer keys as the whiz kid's fingers blurred over his keyboard. "Anything else you need?"

"Yeah, better include some higher grade firepower in the care package Hal's sending down—I don't want to be outgunned in the bush. Give me something carbine size with a collapsible stock, a CAR-15 would do."

"Duly noted. I'll make sure they know to include it and plenty of ammo. You good on everything else?"

"So far, so good. I'll be in touch if I need anything else. Striker out."

Disconnecting the call, Bolan prepped for bed, turning out the light and enjoying the last comfortable bed he expected he'd see for a while. As soon as his head hit the pillow, he was out.

**4**

Alec Hachtman frowned at the water drop that had splashed on his keyboard just as a sharp pain bloomed in his neck. Slapping a hand down, he brought away a crushed mosquito in his fingers and groaned. Looking up, he saw another drop poised to fall, and snatched his laptop out of the way a moment before it plopped onto his lap desk.

Starting to hate the place, he activated the VOIP program on his machine. "Kapleron, my tent is leaking again. Please have one of the locals take a look at it as soon as possible."

"Yeah, but it probably won't do you much good—it's called a *rain*forest for a reason, you know? I'll get someone on it when I can."

"Well, get them on it sooner rather than later, all right? I woke up this morning half-drenched." Hachtman closed his computer and slid it into the protective padded ballistic nylon case that was always nearby. Given their situation, he carried the computer with him at all times, in the event that a hurried evacuation was necessary. Slinging the case strap over his shoulder, he rose from his cot and left the claustrophobic tent, emerging into the muggy, humid Amazon jungle.

Wondering again why he'd agreed to oversee this mission, he mopped his forehead with a handkerchief. *Sure, it'll be exciting—come down to South America! This will be great for your record with the company!* What a load—all that's down here is heat, bugs, more heat and these insufferable goddamn mercenaries whose answer to everything is to point a gun and start blasting. They'd be lucky if the whole goddamn forest wasn't blown up before they'd finished here.

Hachtman was the ostensible leader of the operation for his company, Paracor Security Solutions International, a private military company eking out a living on the fringes of the Second and Third World. With most of the plum operations going to larger, multinational PMCs, Paracor battled for scraps at the bottom, taking boring, out-of-the-way assignments in the ass end of the world. Their board was looking to move the company up the ranks into the leagues of the big boys and were willing to reward those who could help them accomplish this task.

That was why Hachtman was here. He'd volunteered to oversee the mission to "pacify" the area so that it could be parceled out to oil companies, loggers, whomever wanted to turn a buck exploiting the riches of the rainforest. The board had made it known that they wanted a perfect operations record that they could use to burnish their reputation—and Hachtman was going to give it to them. All he needed was a few more days, and he would deliver a successful foiling of renegade Colombian soldiers terrorizing the defenseless natives—and perhaps a nearby prospecting oil company, as well.

That was, if he could survive this infernal jungle that long. The eternal heat, the constant biting insects and the wet that permeated everything had wreaked havoc on his wardrobe, not to mention his computer and other personal effects. After this, he figured he was due a long vacation—maybe somewhere sunny and bright instead of humid and damp all the time.

As he walked toward the trucks, Hachtman spotted his head of security, Piet Kapleron, coming the other way. The short, pale-skinned, bandy-legged, freckled South African stood out among the rest of the hired guns in looks as well as temperament. His disdain for the operation was obvious—he made no bones about what he thought of Hachtman and any other "suit." But he was effective, and that was all that mattered.

"Good afternoon, Piet."

"How goes it, *baas?*" The shorter man fell into step beside him. Kapleron's Afrikanner accent irritated Hachtman, but he was careful not to show it. For all the man's lack of manners, he was good at his job, keeping at bay the potential cauldron of trouble—from nosy relief workers to natives in the wrong place at the wrong time, to local soldiers or militia stumbling upon them and then demanding bribes to keep their mouths shut. Kapleron handled them all, letting Hachtman and his team do their job in relative peace.

"Fine, except my tent's leaking again. How's the perimeter? Any trouble recently?"

"That's what I came to talk to you about. Those bastards at that village nearby are trekkin' closer to us all the time. Pretty soon they'll be stomping all over the place." Kapleron's lip curled at the thought.

"What would you suggest we do about that, keeping in mind that our employers want this operation to keep a low profile?"

"*Ja,* I remember, otherwise the problem woulda been solved already—a few of my *maats* and I woulda paid them a daylight visit. However, since that ain't an option, perhaps a different approach is in order."

"Oh?" Hachtman lengthened his stride, making the shorter man hasten to catch up. It was a faint jab at the other man, but he took his pleasure where he could.

"Yeah, look, apparently these Huaorani are attacking each other all the time—they stab their enemies with spears. We go in at night and take out the village, then it looks like one of the neighbors did it, not us. Just another hazard of living in the jungle, right? The locals all suspect each other, and we get off scot-free. Heh, if you wanted to live on something more than coconuts and guava, we could even hire ourselves out for 'protection.'"

Pondering the rough plan for a moment, Hachtman was

surprised to find he liked it. "That's not a bad idea—it certainly covers all of our bases."

"So, when do you want us to move on them?"

"Let me get back to you on that, okay?" Leaving the small man behind, he headed for a cab on one of the deuce-and-a-half trucks and climbed inside. Unzipping the case again, he connected his laptop to the battery of the truck and extended a small satellite transmitting dish. He drummed his fingers on the dashboard, waiting for the interminable lag as the satellite connection uplinked to his superior at the company.

"Good afternoon, Alec." His boss, known only as Mr. Ravidos, never appeared on screen—the only thing Hachtman saw was the logo of Paracor, two crossed swords on a crimson field.

"Good afternoon, sir."

"I assume you're calling with an update."

"Yes, sir. The first phase of the operation has been carried out, however, there is another village nearby that may need pacifying, as well. We're checking into it right now."

"Of course, you know that PSSI cannot be connected to any sort of wet activity in the area."

"Yes, sir. We'll have this section of jungle cleared and ready for companies to move into in the next five to seven days."

"Good. Now that we have the rights to resell, our sales force is already lining up leasers for that swath. We're making history here, Alec. Not only are we supplying the security for an area, but we're also controlling the rights to exploit it—two income streams off one assignment."

"Well, sir, you've always said that good business is where you find it, right?"

"Excellent memory, Alec. You pull this off smoothly, and there'll be a big promotion for you when you come back to headquarters. You just make sure that there's no one there to raise a stink about it, okay?"

"No problem, sir. By the time Piet and his boys are finished, there won't even be a parrot to squawk about what's going on down here."

**5**

The honk of an automobile horn broke Nancy Kelleson's concentration. She looked down to see the rows of figures swim into focus on the inventory sheet. In every column, red ink was the predominant color.

"Well, I might not have enough food, equipment or field supplies, but at least I've got a few more warm bodies to help out for the time being." She pulled back her damp, blond hair—in the humid heat, it never got completely dry—and secured her ponytail with a leather thong. Rising, she pushed the rough, wooden door of her hut aside and stepped out to meet the new arrivals.

The pair of four-wheel-drive Land Rovers had pulled into the center of the village, surrounded, as always, by the population of the small enclave, about fifty men, women and children. Most were dressed in simple, brightly colored clothes that were a mixture of native and western styles. The children ran around barefoot and either bare-chested or clad in T-shirts and worn shorts. The women dressed in a mix of the traditional breechclout covering, also going bare-breasted. The men wore mainly simple shirts and pants or shorts. Some articles of clothing had been white a long time ago, to protect against the tropical sun, but they had all turned a dirty gray-brown over time.

As usual, Kelleson headed straight for the driver of the first vehicle, a short man with ebony skin, thinning, curly hair and an ever-present smile that revealed one missing front tooth. He directed the other passengers to unload their duffels and for the villagers to remove the supplies they had brought back. "How was the trip, Etienne?"

He looked up at her—the top of his head barely came to her jaw—and held out a stubby-fingered hand, waggling it back and forth. "Not as bad as the last one—we only had to stop six times to clear the road, a new record. At least we didn't break anything this time. I think, however, that Major Medina will be paying a visit here soon—he seemed to be particularly interested in the new arrivals."

"Just what I need right now." Kelleson brushed an errant strand of hair out of her eyes and turned to the half dozen men and women standing to one side, their Caucasian skin, tans and new clothing demarking them as her fresh recruits. "I'm off to give the welcome speech to the newbies."

"Good luck, we'll have this squared away by the time you're finished. Oh, one more thing—the Feri pump finally arrived."

"Finally? Thank God for small favors, I say. I just hope it works as well as they promised. We'll make that a priority— fresh, clean water will go a long way toward making things better around here. Thanks for the great news."

The short man grinned again while hoisting a forty-pound sack of corn with distinctive Red Cross markings over his shoulder. "I bring it all back, good and bad—you know that."

"Yes, I certainly do." Squaring her shoulders, Kelleson approached the small group, noting that most of them looked to be either from Europe or America. She took a moment to watch as they all stared around at the strange new world they had just stepped into. "I trust you all enjoyed the trip here?"

"Sure, if you call twenty hours crammed in five airplanes, followed by an eight-hour drive into the bush enjoyable." The speaker was a tall, rail-thin guy with short, black hair and wire-rimmed glasses. His comment brought weary chuckles from the other three men, a grin from one of the women and a glare from the other one.

"First, let me welcome you to this Huaorani village in the province of Sucumbíos, Ecuador. My name is Nancy Kelleson, and I'm your headperson for this SARE project. Over the next six months, we'll all be helping this village become more self-sufficient, installing a new well, clearing and planting fields and teaching Spanish and English and their country's history to the children." She looked each person directly in the eyes as she spoke. "Make no mistake about it, this is not a vacation or pleasure trip. You all volunteered for SARE with the expectation of seeing the world and working hard, and I can guarantee that you're going to get both in about equal measure."

She extended a hand to encompass the cluster of single-story wooden huts with thatched roofs, all surrounding a cleared main square. In the back of all the houses, looming over all of them, was the thick, verdant jungle. "The first rule I want all of you to take to heart is that the moment you set foot here, you entered hostile territory. The jungle can kill you as easily as breathing. It will swallow you up without mercy, pick your bones clean and leave what's left to bleach in the sun before being covered by the foliage in less than a week. Treat the jungle and its denizens with the respect they deserve—you won't often get a second chance."

All eyes were on Kelleson, the group's shared fatigue forgotten for the moment as she spoke. "The second thing to remember is that we are in a Third World country, so things are done differently here. Always keep your identification papers on you at all times, and do not go anywhere without a native as guide. There are soldiers in the area, some from the Ecuadorian Army, some from the Colombian Army, as we are near the border between the two nations. If you are stopped for any reason, be patient and polite. Sometimes mentioning SARE might get you out of the situation, other times it might cost you some money, if you're lucky. Either one is preferable to spending any time in a South American jail.

"Why don't each of you take a moment to introduce yourself and tell the rest a little about why you decided to come

here?" As each member of the group spoke, Kelleson evalu-
ated them. There was a last-minute arrival with the group, a
tall, well-built man in his late-thirties, with black hair and
ice-blue eyes. He said he was Matt Cooper, a freelance journalist who was here to see how SARE was helping the indigenous population, but his intent gaze put Kelleson's senses on
alert. She'd seen that stare before and it never boded well for
the people around a person like that.

Cooper was definitely older than most of the others,
about Wilberson's age, and also carried himself differently.
Whereas the other members were staring around in surprise
or awe, his gaze had seemed to size up the situation effi-
ciently, almost as if he were checking for escape routes—or
figuring out how to defend the place from an invasion.

Kelleson made a mental note to keep an eye on him as she
addressed the rest of the group again. "It's good to meet all
of you. I imagine you're pretty strung out from the travel, so
the rest of the day is a light one, to give you time to become
acclimated to the area. Two more tips that will make your
stay here a more pleasant one. First, I know they harped on it
during orientation, but I'm going to repeat it again—stay hy-
drated. The temperature here can reach a balmy forty degrees
Celsius—that's more than one hundred-five Fahrenheit—and
you'll sweat more than you might think. Remind yourself to
drink often—and yes, you'll get used to the taste of the chlo-
rinated water soon enough. If the pump for the well works,
there will be better water shortly.

"Second, although I know we're in the rainforest, it can
still be pretty cool here, especially at night. That combined
with rain can cause a chill that could develop into something
worse. Be sure to dress appropriately. That always means
long sleeves and pants when going out into the jungle, as
there are dozens of plants and insects that would like to get a
piece of you. Are there any questions so far?"

Wilberson piped up again. "Where are we sleeping?"

"You're fortunate enough to be staying in my old tents for
the next few weeks, until you build your own hut. It's part of

the reclamation effort to expand the village, so I hope you all know one end of a hammer from the other. Take the rest of the afternoon to look around, introduce yourself and get the lay of the land. Again, do not go off into the jungle by yourself until you know your way around—it is far too easy to get lost here. Come on, I'll take you to your temporary quarters."

As they walked, she noticed Cooper already attracting attention from the children of the village, each of whom would shyly come up and take something from his hand, then dart away with smiles and laughter. When they reached the three surplus Army tents, Kelleson wasn't surprised to see the looks of dismay on the volunteers' faces.

"I know they don't look like much, but the mosquito netting is intact, and trust me, most days you'll be working so hard you won't notice where you're sleeping. Besides, just think of this as incentive to get your hut completed more quickly, right?"

One of the college students—Mike, she thought—pushed back the stained canvas flap with a whistle. "Boy, SARE wasn't kidding when they said we were roughing it."

"No, and even with the Amazon getting more of a priority lately, we're still lucky to have this stuff."

The South American Relief Effort, or SARE, was a small but growing Third World relief organization that had been founded and dedicated solely for providing assistance to the indigenous tribes on the continent. The non-government organization accepted volunteers with diverse skills to help out all across the continent. For Kelleson, it had been the perfect opportunity to escape her checkered past, leaving that old life behind to start fresh, which she had seized with both hands. Once involved, she discovered that she actually liked the amazing stress of helping people better their lives in some of the worst parts of the world. She had been here for three months so far and would stay as long as it took to complete her mission.

Best to at least better break these newbies in so they don't accidentally kill themselves, Kelleson thought as she watched the group sort out who would bunk where. Once again, Cooper stood a few yards away from the rest, and she peeked around a corner of the tent to see him hunkered down in front of even more children, handing something shiny to one of the little girls, who snatched it with a giggle and ran off.

"Already making friends?"

He looked up, then stood to face her. "I heard bringing small gifts for the children here is a great icebreaker. I managed to keep a chocolate bar somewhat intact during the trip, but it melted as fast as I could hand the squares out."

"Yeah, I hope you didn't have any more in your backpack, otherwise you're in for a runny surprise."

A dismayed shout came from inside the tent, and Cooper grinned. "Sounds like one of the others just found that out."

Kelleson was a big believer in being direct, particularly at the moment. "I was a bit surprised to find a journalist coming all the way out here, Matt."

He smiled, a disarming grin that transformed his face from dead serious to something approaching charming. "I hope you don't think of me that way while I'm here—just treat me like any other volunteer, so I can get the full experience. I'm not afraid of work, and I'm game to tackle just about whatever needs doing around here, from installing that well part Etienne told us about on the way over, to building that hut, working with the locals—you know, getting my hands dirty. It makes for a better story back in the world."

"Glad to hear that. A lot of the people who come here don't have any idea just what's involved in keeping a village like this going, so it's good to see at least one of you is prepared. As for the rest, we'll see what happens. Why don't you get your gear stowed—" of the group, he had traveled the lightest, with a frameless backpack and nothing else "—and dinner will be served in about an hour and a half. You'll get your first taste of real Ecuadorian cuisine."

"After that airline food, anything different will be a pleasure." The big American checked his backpack for insects before hoisting it over his shoulder and disappearing into the tent.

Kelleson looked after him, an expression between a smile and puzzlement on her face. There was something about him, she thought, but she couldn't quite put her finger on it. Reaffirming her determination to keep an eye on him, she turned to find Etienne, go through the rest of the new supplies and figure out how to make them last for another month.

**6**

Kelleson blew a tendril of hair out of her face, then sucked down a large gulp of tepid water, barely noticing the chemical taste. Leaning against the Land Rover's mud-spattered fender, she surveyed the bustling village.

The unpacking had gone well, with Cooper and the other guy—what was his name, Morgan?—pitching in to help. Although Kelleson was pretty sure he had been in the country a while, as he seemed far too comfortable. While the others constantly glanced around at the strange sounds of the jungle or stared at the dark-skinned, loose-jointed natives, he moved through it all as if he'd been here for months rather than a day. Another thing about him that doesn't add up, she thought.

The sun was sinking into the western jungle, painting the trees, vines and foliage in shades of red and gold. This was one of her favorite times of the day—the oppressive heat was starting to fade and the inky blackness of night hadn't yet overtaken them. A fire was being started in the central square, the villagers preparing their traditional meal and celebration to welcome the new arrivals.

The smell of cooking meat made her mouth water, and Kelleson pushed off the SUV to amble toward the pit. Spotting Etienne talking with a small group of villagers, she approached slowly, not wanting to be intrusive.

Upon seeing her, the wiry man's face lit up. "Good evening, Nancy."

"Hi, Etienne. What smells so good over here?"

"The elders have been roasting a pig to celebrate the arrival of the volunteers. They'll serve it with yucca fries, rice and stewed vegetables. My mouth is watering just thinking about it. It'll be ready..."

Bright lights flashed from the lone rutted dirt road leading to the village, along with the loud blare of a horn, making villagers start in alarm and kids scatter to the safety of their huts. Kelleson whirled to see a large, six-wheeled armored personnel carrier painted in camouflage green, brown and black roar into the village, its gun ports bristling with assault rifle barrels and a wicked-looking machine gun mounted on top.

The men and women of the village melted away, leaving Etienne and Kelleson alone near the well. She snorted in disgust as the throaty roar of the APC's turbo-diesel made conversation impossible. The engine cut out and the back doors swung open, discharging soldiers in camouflage fatigues and helmets, their Galil ACE rifles held at port arms as they established a defensive perimeter.

"Jesus, he sure has to make an entrance, doesn't he?" Kelleson mused. "I don't see how that beast doesn't get stuck on the road. What is it, ten tons at least?"

Etienne whistled in admiration. "More like twenty. That's an Urutu—made in Brazil. See that angled undercarriage? It's meant to protect the soldiers inside from mines. I wonder whose palm Medina greased to pick up that beauty?"

Kelleson grimaced. "I'll see if I can find out for you."

A man with sergeant's stripes on his camouflaged sleeve checked the placement of the men, then went to the passenger door and knocked on it three times. The door opened and Major Andrés Medina stepped out.

Like his men, the major was dressed in fatigues, but where his men's uniforms were sweat-stained and disheveled from their patrol, his pressed uniform was spotless and his boots were shined to a high gloss. Aviator sunglasses covered his eyes, and a bright blue ascot was carefully knotted around his neck. His unit was part of the *Fuerza de Despliegue Rápido,* or Rapid Deployment Force. They were supposed to carry out operations against insurgents or criminals, but as Major Medina spent more time busting smugglers and running guns, all that meant to Kelleson was that these thugs all wore the same outfit. The first thing she'd learned upon her arrival was that the idea of peace and safety along the border was as illusory as the idea of a protecting army. Anything and anyone was for sale here, and the price was often a single bullet.

Medina was one of thousands of the same kinds of men Kelleson had seen all over the world. He used his position of authority to get what he wanted, whether it was a new vehicle in exchange for allowing smugglers through the province he was supposed to be guarding, or shaking down villagers in exchange for his protection or fining oil drillers or prospectors for imaginary offenses. His hand was always out, and his gaze was always searching. He was quick to offer what the other person first thought was a bargain, only to later find out that Medina's terms always benefited the major much more than his victim in the end.

When he saw Kelleson and Etienne, his mouth split in a wide smile, revealing white, even teeth, one capped in gold. "Ah, my friends, it is good to see you again."

Kelleson smiled in return, showing no teeth. "You're out rather late, Major. What can we do for you?"

"Is there someplace we can talk—privately?" His gaze flicked over Etienne with casual disdain. The shorter man showed no reaction, standing so still he might have been carved from one of the nearby trees.

"Of course. Please, come into my hut." Kelleson led the way, knowing the officer was watching her ass as she walked. She moved the blanket aside and hung it on the peg to let the waning light in through the doorway. When Medina moved the blanket back to block the opening, the first tremor of alarm tensed her body. Like most men here, he viewed her as exotic—there simply weren't many white women around, save for the two new arrivals—and she knew he had designs on her. Vowing to have that talk with the girls tomorrow, she decided that in the meantime, she could use it to her advantage—carefully.

"Something to drink? I have a bit of tea left."

Medina carefully took off his beret, rolled it and slipped it through his shoulder epaulet before sitting in the chair. "No, thank you, I cannot stay long. We have another village to visit before heading back and the roads out here…" He shrugged, silently acknowledging that they wouldn't improve in either of their lifetimes.

"Of course. So, why are you here?" Kelleson didn't add that her village was about fifty kilometers off Medina's normal patrol grounds—she didn't want him to know she had been keeping tabs on his movements.

"My superiors have reassigned me closer to your village." Medina glanced over his shoulder at the doorway. "Have you heard anything unusual happening in the area? Any of the other villages nearby reporting strange events?"

"Major, the nearest village is a half day's drive away—we're lucky if we see anyone from outside the area once a month."

"Then I take it that's a no."

"You're correct. What are you referring to? Are the rebels recruiting again?" That was one of Kelleson's biggest fears—that one of the groups in the area would sweep through the village on a raid to bolster their numbers. Although FARC and other splinter groups preferred to have willing members, they weren't above kidnapping kids and young men and indoctrinating them into the cause.

"No, nothing so simple. If that were the case, my men and I would have taken care of them already."

Kelleson kept a straight face at the soldier's boast; she knew he was working with half the militias in the area, trading arms for information, gold, cocaine, whatever he needed.

The rest he had either already double-crossed, wiped out or had working for him without their knowledge. "Of course you would have. So, tell me—" sitting on her rough table, Kelleson crossed her arms under her chest and leaned forward "—what's this all about?"

She had to give him credit—Medina's eyes only strayed for a second before fixing on her face again. "This involves the safety of the village, and I want you to keep what I am about to say to yourself—there is no need to scare the people here."

Kelleson nodded. "You have my word that I will be discreet."

"No one around here has mentioned anything about strange events in their village—an entire population disappearing or getting killed all at once?"

Kelleson smiled and quickly wiped it off her face. "If you didn't look so serious, I'd think you were trying to just scare me. I don't recall hearing any such stories. Are you saying the villagers here could be in danger?"

"That is what I have been sent to find out. With the improvements we have been making in the area, we do not want ridiculous tales to be coming out of here, undermining our efforts."

"Naturally you wouldn't want that." Unless it somehow served his purposes, Kelleson thought. "How can I help?"

"We'll be patrolling in the area for the next few weeks, so any information that you might learn would be very helpful. Even with the natives supposedly in a state of war, they still manage to spread stories like wildfire." He stood and walked over to Kelleson, who resisted the urge to shrink back. "I want to make sure you and those volunteers are safe, as well. It wouldn't be good for anyone to get hurt while out here."

A veiled threat or an honest offer of assistance? Nancy played it safe. "The volunteers know the risks when they come out here. However, I appreciate that you'll be looking out for us, and if anything strange is happening out here, I'll be sure to inform you of anything I might find out."

The officer's dark brown eyes bored into Kelleson's blue ones. "I would be happy to do so much more—for you and the village, if you wish."

There it is, she mused, and played dumb. "Well, we've been trying to get more supplies from the larger aid groups in the area, but it's been slow going. Perhaps you could assist with the paperwork on that—you know, speed things up a bit."

"I can look into that." Medina reached out and placed his hand on her arm. "And what is it that you need, Nancy?"

"We could also use a solar panel for the shortwave radio. The batteries just keep dying in this heat—we're lucky to get a few hours out of them."

Medina placed his other hand on Nancy's opposite arm. He smelled not unpleasant; a mixture of some kind of cologne and the ever-present sweat that everyone gave off in this heat. "No, Nancy—what do *you* need?"

Kelleson reached up and gently removed his hands from her body. "Right now I need to do my job and make sure these villagers—and the new volunteers—are taken care of."

"Hmm." Medina turned away and studied her hut as if he was suddenly interested in the surroundings. "Yes, you have done much during your short time here. It would be a shame if that were to come to an end."

"I don't follow you."

He whirled back to her, suddenly only inches away from her face. Kelleson didn't move, although her leg twitched. She stilled it before she did something she wouldn't be able to take back. "I know much about you, Ms. Nancy Kelleson. I know where you come from and why you're here."

"What are you talking about? I came here to help—"

"You came here because you didn't have much choice. I know about the private school in England and the reason you left—"

Kelleson's hand blurred to slap him, but Medina was quicker and grabbed her wrist before the blow could land. "Now, now, that's no way to treat the person who's going to keep your little secret, is it? There's no need for the villagers to know about your little *indiscretion*. It would be too bad if the women here found out the real reason you left your homeland and came here. You know how closed-minded they are—after all, you did it once already, who knows when you might do it again and to whom? No one would trust you, would they? Your time here would quickly be at an end, wouldn't it?"

"I made a mistake and now I'm trying to start my life over again. You had no right— My past is none of your business…" Kelleson fought to keep tears filling her eyes from spilling down her cheeks.

"Oh, I beg to differ. As I am responsible for the safety of the people here, it is very much my business—"

A knock on the side of the hut made Medina and Kelleson both turn toward the doorway, where the blanket was swept aside to reveal one of the new volunteers standing there.

"Nancy, I was—oh, I'm sorry, am I interrupting?" Kelleson noticed Cooper's eyes narrow as he took in the scene in front of him, his body tensing and his hands clenching into loose fists. "Is something wrong?"

Kelleson wiped at her eyes with her sleeve. "No. Major Medina was…was just leaving."

"Quite." The immaculate soldier leaned close to her. "Think carefully about what we spoke of today. Perhaps when I return in a few days to talk again, you'll be more amenable to…working together more closely." Snatching his beret from his shoulder, he put it on, adjusting the cloth cap just so, and stalked out of the hut, shouldering the big American out of the way.

The solidly built man easily regained his balance and reappeared in the opening. "Are you all right?"

Using the brief distraction caused by Medina's exit to recompose herself, Kelleson glanced at him with a brief smile. "Fine, Cooper, thanks. The major takes his job very seriously, and he was just making sure I understood that."

"Really?" The dark-haired man's expression indicated that

he didn't believe Kelleson's excuse for a moment. "It looked more like he was threatening you, or maybe shaking you down for something. Was he asking for a bribe—or something else?"

"No, no, it's not what you think at all. The people here have a very different way of doing things, and some of them aren't quite as politically correct as you or I might wish, that's all. I appreciate your concern, but please, don't worry about it—I'm fine, really."

"All right, if you say so. Dinner's ready, and Etienne asked me to come get you, he mentioned something about participating in a welcoming ceremony."

"Ah, good, they're ready. I hope you don't have two left feet, Cooper. The celebration welcoming all of you features singing and dancing and eating a lot of what you and the others might consider very strange food."

"Stranger than the bull penis soup I had yesterday?" He smiled. "As long as there's plenty of it, I should be all right."

She walked to the doorway and looked him up and down. "There will be, but do me and the rest of the group a favor and have at least one bite of each meal, all right? It would be an insult to the village if you refused their generosity this evening. They don't cook food like this without feeling the cost to their families."

He grimaced. "Then perhaps they shouldn't do it—after all, we came from America, where we invented the concept of the 'fourth meal,' despite the fact that hundreds of millions of people around the world are lucky to get one or two. In my opinion, there's no need to impress us with this."

Kelleson fixed him with an appraising look. "Did you ever consider that it might not be as much about impressing you as it is the collective pride of the village to be able to do this in the first place?"

Bolan took that in and nodded. "Touché. All right, I'll nod and smile with the rest of them."

"Thanks. Now let's eat." Slipping her arm through his, Kelleson led him to the bright fire and the drumming, clapping, singing villagers in the square.

**7**

In the dead of the night, Bolan's eyes popped open without the aid of an alarm or light. He lay still for a moment, letting his senses come alive to sift the various night sounds, from the breathing noises of his tent mates to the cacophony of the insect nightlife.

Everyone around him was out cold, from the slight snore of the two college boys to the Tatrow woman, who sounded angry even while she slept.

Bolan rose from his cot and exited the mosquito netting, heading for the tent flap. Once there, he paused for a moment as one of the volunteers shifted on their bunk, mumbling softly to themselves. Bolan caught a snatch of one of the tribal chants they'd learned earlier that evening.

With a smile, he poked his head out of the tent and looked around. The gibbous moon cast its silver light on the jungle, turning the tall trees and thick ground foliage into a ghostly, silver-shaded landscape. The scent of the wonderful meal, mingled with the lingering aroma of wood smoke, still hung over the area. The villagers had also gone to bed after the welcome celebration, and silence reigned over the huts where there had been chants, shouts and laughter earlier that evening.

For living in the middle of nowhere, these folks sure know how to party, Bolan thought as he slipped out of the tent and into the tree line, skirting the perimeter until he reached the

northwestern part of the clearing. The feast and dancing had
been an unexpected treat, with the food being plentiful and
tasty—the roast pig was some of the best he'd ever tasted,
and there were also plenty of other dishes, including roasted
tapir and monkey, to go around. Kelleson had made a small
speech welcoming the group to both South America and the
village, and the chief of the village also spoke, welcoming
the *cowodi,* or outsiders. The after-dinner entertainment had
been singing, provided by the villagers.

Bolan had enjoyed the festivities, finding them a pleasant diversion from his real mission. Of course, he was still
keeping tabs on everything, from noticing how the thinner
college boy was cozying up to Calley Carter—he figured
there would be a relationship there soon enough—and the
hungry look in Susanna Tatrow's eyes at the various cou-
ples around the campfire, which was quickly hidden under
her haughty veneer. Bolan also made sure to keep an eye
on Elliot Morgan, as well, who ate well and seemed to be
the most at ease with the natives—a sign that he'd been in
country longer than he claimed. He also stole more than one
glance at Kelleson, who joined in the party with what looked
like good-humored cheer, but remained distant and pensive
throughout the evening. Although Bolan was well aware of
the priority of his mission, at the same time he felt for her and
the situation she was in, and was going to see if there was
anything he could do for her—as long as it didn't break his
cover, of course.

Speaking of cover, it's time to get to work, he thought.
Taking out his smartphone, he turned it on and saw a message. Your package has been delivered by SMF Express.

It was followed by a set of coordinates. Grinning, since it
had to be Tokaido who'd sent the message, Bolan activated
a program that used satellite coverage to sketch in a small
map of the area and revealed a red, blinking dot about three
miles away—his goal for the evening. Committing the route
to memory, he pocketed the smartphone.

Rolling down the sleeves of his shirt and pants to cover

his arms and legs, he wrapped a black silk scarf around his head, glanced around one last time to make sure no one was watching, then loped into the jungle, machete in hand.

Well versed in the dangers of the rainforest, Bolan stuck to a game trail that would take him most of the way to his target, but there would be a 500-yard stretch where he'd leave the trail and head into the forest to retrieve his package. The trip back should be easier, he thought, with the NVGs that turn darkness into daylight. He was armed, but it wasn't nearly enough to fend off a curious or hungry jungle predator. Instead, he had to move fast and then hope nothing fixed on him as a potential meal before he could get to his air-dropped cache.

A rustle in the brush to his right made him freeze, eyes scanning the silver-black foliage for signs of movement, ears straining for the smallest sound. His left hand stole down to the back of his pants and drew the SIG Sauer 9 mm pistol there, flipping off the safety and placing a finger on the trigger. The brush rustled again and the bushes parted to reveal the face of a jaguar peering out at him.

Bolan stayed perfectly still, as he knew the great cat might chase him down if he ran. He didn't want to shoot the animal—it was only doing what came naturally, and besides, the shot would definitely be heard in the camp, making his return problematic.

Inch by inch, he slowly raised the pistol while keeping his eyes on the animal through his top peripheral vision. Slowly he crouched and took aim, eyes averted so he didn't spook the animal. For a moment the two regarded each other, then the jaguar—a magnificent black and spotted creature the size of a full-grown lioness—half turned, as if it heard something coming down the trail. With barely a sound, it vanished into the underbrush, leaving Bolan to breathe a sigh of relief.

But his reprieve quickly turned to alarm as he also heard the sound of something else moving toward him. Whatever it was, it was making too much noise to be another animal, and he caught the low murmur of human voices.

With no better place to go, he safetied the SIG and tucked it at his back as he stepped into the space the jaguar had just vacated. Hunkering down, he rearranged the nearby fronds and plants to conceal himself from whoever was approaching.

Could it be poachers out here at this hour, he wondered, curling into a tight ball and pulling the brush closer to him. He left a small opening to observe the trail just as four dark figures appeared about ten yards away.

*Shit.*

Any doubts he had about their intentions were dispelled by their appearance—tiger-stripe camouflage, combat boots and boonie hats. Each one carried a long-barreled rifle, but they looked strange to Bolan's eye—not assault rifles, but heavy-duty dart guns.

The squad halted as the leader held up his fist, then signaled for one to creep ahead to the left and another to the right. Each man moved with silent precision, letting Bolan know he was up against either professional hunters or men with military experience.

With nowhere to go, all he could do was pretend to be a motionless rock and hope they didn't investigate the brush too closely. The man on the left was coming closer with each step, his attention fixed on the ground in front of him. Bolan took out a small canister from one of his pockets, making sure it was ready to spray. The man was only about four yards away—three—two yards—

Bolan brought his right arm up and prepared to blast the guy full in the face.

A crackle in the brush behind him made everyone freeze, heads swiveling toward the noise. The man almost on top of him turned to face it, then stepped into the deeper brush, flanked by the leader, with their rear guard becoming the rightmost hunter. The man who had gone off to the left brought up the rear, about ten yards behind the other three. Unfortunately, he took the straightest route across the trail— which would lead him directly into Bolan.

As he cleared the fronds away with his rifle barrel, Bolan saw the man's eyes widen in surprise as he came across what looked like a small hillock, but which quickly uncoiled and pointed a small aerosol can at him. Even as Bolan squeezed the trigger, the man brought his rifle around while ducking out of the way of the stream, which caught him on the side of the face. The volatile oleoresin capsicum mixture caused his eyes to immediately swell and water and his throat to close. However, the man still had enough presence of mind to try to shout for help, gasping for enough breath to do so as Bolan leaped at him, trying to tackle him and cover his mouth.

Even partially incapacitated by the spray, the hunter stepped back and brought the butt of his rifle around. The clumsy swing smacked Bolan on his arm, sending a jolt of pain up into his shoulder. Then he was on the man, crushing him to the ground and driving the breath from his lungs. However, the rifle was caught between them and the man used it to try to lever Bolan off, writhing and shoving while trying to suck in a breath. He partially succeeded, pushing his opponent to one side.

Bolan drove his elbow into the man's nose, feeling cartilage and bone crunch under the blow. The man grunted as his head snapped back, bouncing off the ground. Bolan followed up with a palm strike to the man's temple, which stopped his struggling immediately, his limp limbs flopping to the ground.

Snatching up the rifle, Bolan whirled and aimed it where the other men had disappeared into the jungle, expecting one of them to burst out of the underbrush at any moment. Although the fight had taken less than five seconds, it had felt like an hour, and he thought they'd made enough noise to attract anyone within five miles. When no one came to investigate, he broke the rifle's action, extracted the dart and threw it into the brush, and crept away, heading down the trail in the direction the men had come from.

He kept going for three minutes, then tossed the rifle into the brush and whipped out his phone to get his bear-

ings. Once he knew where he was, he stepped carefully off
the trail, making sure not to leave any obvious trace of his
passage, and headed north, planning to angle over as he got
closer to the waiting package. His arm still throbbed from
where he'd been struck, but Bolan knew it would be all right;
the blow hadn't hit bone, just muscle.

Along the way, even though he remained alert, a part of
his mind turned over what he'd just seen. Most poachers preferred to work in daylight, operating out of SUVs on the sa-
vannah, where they could evade the thinly spread soldiers or
park rangers in the area. But these guys were on foot, hunting
at night, with dart guns—wanting to capture their prey alive.
It would seem, Bolan thought, that they weren't after skins
or trophies. They want the animals themselves—reselling to
private zoos or European billionaires?

Try as he might, he couldn't come up with an answer.
Although he didn't think he was being followed, Bolan executed an intricate trail through the jungle, doubling back on
his trail, zigzagging back and forth through the foliage and
looping around more than once. After an hour's hard travel,
he reached the drop zone coordinates and was pleased to find
a package dangling from a tree by the ropes of a small parachute.

He observed the site for another ten minutes, making sure
no one was watching, then found a long stick and poked the
tightly bound package, testing for booby traps. It wouldn't
be above the rebels or even the soldiers here to leave a "gift"
for the intended recipient if they'd found this first. Of course,
if they had tried to open it, they would have gotten a nasty
surprise themselves, he thought as he aimed his smartphone
at the bundle and texted a four-digit code. A soft beep con-
firmed that the built-in deterrent—two ounces of Semtex
wrapped in a thin layer around his supplies—was currently
unarmed. Only then did he cut the package down and unwrap
it. He separated the radio detonator, wadded up the plastic
explosive and wrapped it in the plastic, stowing it in a side
pocket of his cargo pants.

The weapons were the first item he reviewed. Holding up a matte-black M-4 5.56 mm carbine, Bolan quickly checked the action and inserted one of the four included magazines before slinging it across his back. There were more magazines for his SIG and a silencer for the pistol. Even though Stony Man Farm probably could have gotten the rifle and equipment to him by more conventional means, the chances of it being spotted during his trip out with the other volunteers was too high to risk. It was an expensive air drop, but the gear was worth it.

The next item he unpacked made Bolan smile. State-of-the-art night-vision goggles would give him the edge over just about anyone out here. He checked the small battery pack and the solar-recharging unit and was relieved to find them both undamaged.

Slipping the goggles on his head, he turned them on, the forest turning from black to light green as the fourth-generation night-vision technology activated. This version had a few more features added to it, including the ability to detect across multiple spectrums such as heat and motion, and a heads-up display that relayed current latitude and longitude, and a wireless connection to his sat phone that displayed current geographic information, including the best route back to the village.

Bolan glanced around to make sure no one else was creeping up on him, then sorted through what other items had been sent. Brognola had also included a small first-aid kit containing, among other things, sedatives, antiseptic cream and antidotes for some of the more exotic diseases and poisons he might encounter. Bolan hadn't arrived in country without his immunizations being up-to-date, but these might come in handy for other people. The Huaorani used curare as a poison on their blowgun darts, and he didn't want to get caught unprepared. The Farm had also included energy food, small, highly concentrated protein bars that would double his energy for approximately eight hours, without the letdown or crash that usually came after. On the other end of the spec-

trum, six Modafinil pills, small tablets that would enable
him to stay awake—and alert—for up to seventy-two hours
without loss of concentration. Bolan pocketed those, fighting
the urge to take one right then and there. It all fit in a small
included pack.

He took down the parachute and concealed it beneath
the underbrush, then checked the time—three hours to get
back to the village before his absence would be noticed.
He brought up the best route back to the game trail, then
switched the vision sensor suite to night vision with an
overlay of heat to alert him to anyone moving in the jungle.
Threading the silencer onto the barrel of the SIG Sauer, he
jacked a shell into the chamber and started creeping back
through the jungle.

Bolan plotted a route that would safely bypass the site
where he had encountered the hunters, although he almost
wanted to go back and track them to find out exactly what
they were up to. But the more logical part of him prevailed,
and he struck out for the trail and the village. There'd be time
to find out what they were up to later, and also whether they
were related to his primary mission.

As he approached the village, his arm was sore from hacking his way through the jungle and he was covered in sweat
as the morning heat rose. It had actually gotten to where he
could see without the help of the NVGs, which he slipped off
and stowed before going any farther. He also found a secure
hiding place for the M-4, camouflaging it with palm leaves
to ensure it was hidden. When he was finished, he found a
hidden copse of trees and called in, getting Brognola himself.

"Striker, good to hear your voice. How's the jungle treat-
ing you?"

"Oh, you know, Hal—you guys send me to some interesting places. I've been in the village since 1520 hours, getting the lay of the land and meeting the other volunteers in
this group. Your intel was right, there's some strange stuff
going down here, although I don't quite have a handle on it
yet. I need background files on one Nancy Kelleson, SARE

volunteer, and also Major Andrés Medina, part of the Rapid Deployment Force in the Colombian Army."

"Colombia?" Brognola broke in. "What the hell are they doing crossing the border like this? After that debacle in '08, are they trying to escalate a full-scale border war again?"

"I didn't get the chance to ask him, but I will the next time I see him." Bolan's tone turned serious. "The best way to him might be through this Kelleson woman—I saw him trying to shake her down in private. It looked like he wanted more than money, so that might be useful leverage later. The natives haven't been very forthcoming, either. I'll keep poking around. Thanks for the care package, by the way—I have a feeling it's gonna come in handy."

"No problem, Striker. Unless something comes up, let's plan on reports every twelve hours."

"All right. Anything else for me?"

"One other thing, you've got at least one PMC operator in the area, probably working for one of the oil surveying companies."

"That explains that—I've already got him pegged, Hal. The guy's name is Elliot Morgan, an alias, I'm sure. I'm uploading pics of him and the other two right now. He didn't sit right from the get-go and that's probably why. The strange thing is, he came along as one of the volunteers, so he's also working undercover."

"What, you think we've got a monopoly on the idea? You know the drill."

"Yeah, find out as much as I can without blowing my cover or getting killed—which, I've gotta say, looks pretty easy to do here, and not just from the natives or soldiers. Don't worry, I'm on it."

"I know you are, Striker. Keep in contact and good luck. Stony Man out."

Smoothing his perspiration-slicked hair back, he then walked to within a few yards of the village clearing and paused to look around, scanning for anyone who might have been watching. When he didn't see anyone, he stepped out, brushing off bits of leaf and muck he had accumulated during his nighttime trek.

He had almost made it back to his tent when the flap of the second one pushed open and Morgan stepped out. "Hey, you're up early."

"Yeah, darn mosquitoes were driving me crazy, so I thought I'd get up and take a walk around—head into the jungle a bit, see what's around."

"Remember, you gotta be careful out there. Lots of animals and natives running around here. Either'd kill you without a second thought, take whatever you got—or eat you—and leave you to rot."

Bolan eyed him speculatively. "You seem to know a lot about the area. Have you been here before?"

Morgan shook his head. "Nope, but I keep my eyes and ears open. They were talking at the airport about the increased violence in the jungles. Just thought I'd give you a friendly warning."

"Thanks for the tip. Hey, I'm starved, wanna go see what's for breakfast?"

"Sounds good."

Bolan wasn't fooled for a moment by Morgan's demeanor. He knew the man was here for something—but what? Even worse, he was pretty sure he hadn't fooled the other man with his alibi about the early morning walk, either. If anything, he looked as if he knew exactly where Bolan had been and what he'd been up to.

And that worried him most of all—not because Bolan was in any danger, but because he just might have to kill the other man before all of this was over.

## 8

Who does this guy think he's kidding?

Morgan watched Cooper out of the corner of his eye as they headed over to eat. Walk in the jungle, my ass, he thought. The fit, muscled freelance journalist, or whatever the hell he was, was sweating as though he'd just finished a 5K race, and his boots and pant legs were soaked to the knee—not like he had just brushed against some wet plants, but like he had been walking through a lot of them in a hurry. Morgan had also noticed the small carryall bag the other man was sporting, too. He was pretty sure the man hadn't had it when he'd arrived yesterday and was itching to see what might be inside.

All in all, Morgan thought, this guy was as fishy as a mackerel in the Sahara. The questions are—what's he doing here and is he going to be a problem, or is he already part of the problem?

The cooking fire was already hot as they approached, sending a tendril of white smoke into the air. Two women tended a large skillet over a blazing fire, its contents sizzling merrily. The smell of oil and what might have been fried green bananas filled the air.

Kelleson stood to one side, arms crossed, deep in conversation with Etienne. When she noticed the two men, she smiled and nodded to them. "Hello, gentlemen."

They both greeted her in English. Elliot spoke fluent Portuguese and Spanish, but there was no need to let them know that just yet. Instead, he went with a classic opener. "What's for breakfast?"

"Glad you asked, the women are making a large batch of *patacones,* to eat with last night's leftovers. Both of you can give them a hand, as the plantains are just about done." She nodded at Etienne, who addressed the women, his words making them smile and nod vigorously.

The men exchanged uneasy looks. "I think we just got volunteered for something," Morgan muttered.

Cooper grimaced. "Yeah, and it's probably not a lot of fun, either." The two men watched as the woman removed the pan from the fire and swiftly flipped the fried slices of plantain onto a large plate.

"All right, mash the slices to half their original height, then the pieces get fried a second time."

Morgan peered at the gleaming lumps of vegetable. "No disrespect intended, but isn't this women's work?"

Kelleson handed him an empty glass soda bottle. "Use the bottom of this. Normally, yes, it is so-called women's work, but in SARE, we like to have the volunteers experience every aspect of a villager's life—it gives you a better appreciation of what these people do every day just to eat."

Morgan squashed the plate of plantain slices down, then slid them back into the oil. The women filled the plate again and Cooper took a turn at it, as well. The two men each did another full plate apiece, then the women signaled for them to stop, nodding in approval.

Off their nod, Kelleson spoke up. "All right, gentlemen, you're done—good work. The stew from last night is over there, as well as what's left from the pig and tapirs, too. Before you eat, however, let's all bow our heads as the elders say grace, shall we?"

Although not a particularly religious man, Morgan lowered his head and listened as one of the older men, his beard heavily salt-and-pepper, led the village in prayer.

He glanced over at Kelleson to see her mouthing different

words, and made out enough of them to understand that she was reciting the Lord's Prayer. He wasn't surprised—a lot of the volunteers he saw in the Third World bush embraced Christianity to one degree or another. He'd found a pair of Jehovah's Witnesses down in South Africa last year, trying to spread the good word among all the violence erupting against the flood of refugees from strife-ridden Zimbabwe. They hadn't been nearly as attractive as Kelleson, however.

The prayer finished, the villagers lined up for breakfast. Each one took a few *patacones,* mashed the center of them with their thumb to create a small hollow and then used it as a makeshift bowl to fill with leftover meat and other food. Morgan followed suit, hanging back until Kelleson got in line, then came up behind her.

"Mr. Morgan. Pretty good technique on those plantains."

"Call me Elliot, and yeah, it was kind of fun once you got the hang of it. I wouldn't want to do that every morning, however, so I hope you've got something a little more challenging lined up for the rest of the day."

Kelleson reached into the pan and assembled her portion with ease. "I think we can find enough around here to keep you occupied. For example, if you know anything about mechanical devices, Etienne could use your help installing the new pump part. The water's getting fairly low here, and I don't like sending the villagers out to the river—it's an hour-long round trip."

"Ouch. Yeah, I'd be glad to pitch in—after all, that's what I'm here for. Say, is there anything else you need?"

Kelleson's head snapped up, and she turned on him so fast Elliot half raised his free hand in case he needed to ward her off. Then, as quickly as she had turned, the fierce expression on her face melted away, and she took a large bite of her *patacones* before replying. "Thanks, but just the fact that you're here to help in the first place is plenty. If you'll excuse me, I have a lot to attend to, including getting the other volunteers situated." She strode away without a backward glance, leaving a slightly befuddled Morgan in her wake.

What the hell was that all about? he wondered, glancing around to see if anyone had been watching. Sure enough, off to one side, Cooper met his gaze as he munched on his breakfast. Morgan saluted him with his own, then ate the surprisingly tasty meal—although the volunteer organization had said each person was guaranteed three meals a day, they'd never described the quality of the food.

After eating, he cleaned off his hands as best as he could, then walked to the vented pit toilet that was set several yards away from the rest of the huts and tents. He stepped inside, both to relieve himself and to make a personal call.

He made sure no one was around, then he seated himself on the simple wooden board above the pit, making sure to breathe through his mouth. He pulled out his satellite phone, turned it on and hit a speed-dial number.

A calm voice answered in a Southern drawl. "Security."

"This is Elliot, I'm on site, and have been for the past sixteen hours."

"'Bout time you reported in. We were startin' to think the bush got ya."

Morgan grinned in spite of his morning. "You'll never be that lucky. So far, nothing out of the ordinary. This village is just like any one of a dozen within a hundred miles. One thing, though—the local army major dropped in himself to visit with the head volunteer here. They had what looked like an interesting conversation, and I think he'll be coming back soon. There's still the possibility he's involved in local criminal activity."

Morgan's contact chuckled. "You still worryin' that one, even after we tol' you that dog won't hunt? Unless you learn otherwise, we're treatin' him as on the level—at least, as much as one of them soldiers can be—so enlist him, bribe him or pump him for info, whichever gits us answers the fastest. The board's getting very antsy to move forward with the upcoming projects, we need to make sure that jungle is clear—there can't be any unknown hazards."

"I hear you, and I'll get to the bottom of this one way or

the other. Hey, also, see what you can find out about Nancy Kelleson. She's that lead volunteer I mentioned—might be an expatriate Brit, she's got an accent. Also, pull anything you can find on a Major Andrés Medina of the Colombian Army. He seems to be the unofficial 'protector' of the area, and is putting pressure on the indigenous population. Let me know what you get as soon as you do—I could use some leverage on both of them."

"This Medina name sounds familiar." Morgan heard computer keys click in the background. "Anything else?"

"Yeah, we picked up a last-minute addition to the group— some hotshot freelance journalist named Matt Cooper. I'm sending a picture of him now. Every time I'm near him, he sets off my bullshit detector. Also, he moves like an ex-military man. Lemme know what you find out on him, too."

"We'll send you whatever we find out on any of them."

"Great. All right, I'd better go—I'm surprised half the village isn't knocking down the toilet door yet. I'll call back about the same time tomorrow."

"Right—and good luck."

Morgan hung up, finished his business and stepped out of the latrine. As he stowed his phone, he half expected to see Cooper spying on him from behind a tree. The area was deserted, however, and he trekked back to the village with ease, where he found the other man huddled with Etienne and a few other men around a three-meter-long plastic pipe that Morgan recognized immediately.

"Hey, that's a Feri pump, isn't it?"

Etienne's eyebrows raised in surprise. "You've seen this before?"

"Seen it, hell, I've installed them down south. You guys picked the right piece of equipment out here—it has only two moving parts, is durable as hell and can even run dry without getting damaged. Where's your compressor and the bore? We can have this sucker up and running in less than thirty minutes if everything else is ready."

Etienne hefted one end of the tube and Morgan grabbed the other. "Nice and light, too. Lead the way, man."

The smaller man headed toward the other end of the village with Morgan in tow. Realizing this might be the opportunity he'd been waiting for, he searched for a reason to get the reporter out of his hair.

As if in answer to his dilemma, Kelleson shouted from across the compound, making both men's heads turn. "Mr. Cooper?"

"Yeah?"

"Time for you to get your hands dirty—come with me to the livestock."

Morgan hid his jubilation. "Have a good time."

The dark-haired man took his comment at face value as he ambled off. "You, too."

All right, Elliot thought as he hefted his end of the pump again. Let's get to work.

Etienne led him to the side of the village farthest away from the pit toilet and, Morgan noted with approval, several feet higher than the latrine, although he supposed the pit could still contaminate the ground water. When he asked Etienne about the possibility, the Ecuadorian shook his head.

"When SARE installed the toilet, they also put in a concrete sewer pit. Nancy's been working with us to transform the waste into useful compost, eliminating the bacteria that might live in it so we can raise better crops. She calls it 'humanure.'"

"Sounds lovely." Banishing the unpleasant thought from his mind, Morgan examined the setup Etienne'd be working with. The bore was a simple hole in the ground, but the villagers had scrounged up a tall length of HDPE pipe to serve as a sleeve to attach the hose to so it would stay in place. On a raised platform next to the hole was a diesel generator for power, with an air compressor to move the water. "How deep is your aquifer?"

"A tributary of the Amazon flows through the region, so we only had to drill down about forty yards." Etienne's teeth flashed in the morning sun as he smiled. "A good thing, too, since the drill broke once it had gotten that far."

"Common problem, that?"

Etienne shrugged. "Out here, things work until they don't, and we fix what we can using parts from what we can't."

"Sounds about right. All right, let's get this set up." Morgan hooked up the air compressor hose to the nozzle on the top of the pump and worked the flexible water hose onto the end next to it, spinning a plastic coupling on to lock the tube down. "Okay, let's put it in. Why don't you set up those guys to make sure the hose doesn't kink as we drop it down?"

Etienne snapped out orders, and the two men grabbed the hose. With the wiry Ecuadorian on one side, Morgan inserted the bottom of the pump into the sleeve and was gratified to find that it fit just right. Hand over hand, they lowered it into the bore, feeding it down, until they met resistance. Morgan pushed down once more, but felt the pump stop moving, and knew they were at the right level. "That's it. All we need to do is secure the hose and fire up the generator, and it should be ready to go."

They did both tasks, a process that took less than five minutes, then Etienne told the other two men to gather the villagers around so they could see the pump work. The pair ran off, leaving Morgan alone with Etienne.

"Should we test it while they're gone?" Etienne asked. "Just to make sure it works?"

Elliot glanced at him. "Is there water down there?" The other man nodded. "Does your generator and compressor work?" Another nod. "Then it'll work, trust me."

"I hope you're right. We're the pilot project for this entire region, so if we get it working, then other villages will follow."

Morgan rubbed his jaw. "Speaking of the other villages, I heard someone in the city saying something about legends of ghosts in the rainforest. Thing was, he didn't sound like he was talking about local legends—it sounded like he was really scared of some kind of spirits in the jungle. Have you heard anything like that recently?"

As Morgan spoke, he watched Etienne's face turn from open and friendly to closed and grave. "Have you asked any of the other villagers about this?"

It was Elliot's turn to shrug. "I don't speak the language, remember?"

"Right, well, do us a favor and don't. There's no need to spook anyone here—their lives are hard enough as it is."

"So there is something going on in the jungle?"

Etienne glanced around before answering. "Lately the more isolated villagers have reported in, such as they can, about disappearing people—men, women, children. The military keeps claiming they'll investigate, but so far nothing has happened. Rumors have it that a patrol went out to investigate one such claim, and none of the soldiers returned—they simply disappeared. It hasn't affected this village yet, and Nancy and I are keeping track of the reports, making sure they don't come too close."

"Pretty risky, to put foreigners in possible harm's way like that, don't you think?"

"No more so than dropping them in the middle of the jungle, don't you think? Besides, there are always ways to die out here, more from nature than man. Your volunteers were made aware of the risks when they came. These 'ghosts' of yours, who knows if they are real, or something made up by the locals—either of which is possible."

"But if people are really disappearing…"

Etienne frowned. "People, even natives, disappear each year in the jungle, and not all of them are found. There are many reasons for this—sneaking off to the cities, stumbling across criminals who don't want witnesses to their deeds, or the rainforest itself claiming a life. We'd need some kind of real proof—not just native stories—before we could do anything about it, or even bring it to the attention of the proper authorities."

"I see. Would it be all right if I asked Nancy about it?"

"What's your interest in these...stories?"

Morgan cracked a smile. "Self-preservation, for one thing. But if someone really is body snatching out here, I think we ought to know about it."

"Rumors, only, keep in mind. But yes, I think you could discuss it with Nancy. Let her know that you spoke to me first, please."

"Naturally—it'll probably keep my head on my shoulders."

Now Etienne's affable grin returned. "Yours and mine both. Here they come."

The two men had done their job well—fully half the village trailed behind them, from the elderly to small children, who had been let out of class to witness what would hopefully be a life-changing event. Kelleson was there, along with Susanna, her kinky hair pulled back and her white skin sweat-streaked and glistening.

After a brief discussion between Morgan and Etienne as to who would do the honors—each wanted the other man to do it—the smaller man stepped forward. "Today marks a new dawn for our village. For today—" Etienne hit the switch on the generator, causing it to roar to life and activate the air compressor "—we have our own water!"

All eyes, including Morgan's, turned toward the pipe that hung a few feet above the ground. The generator hummed and for a moment nothing happened.

Morgan hoped he'd hooked everything up right as a nervous twinge shot through his stomach.

Then, a dribble of brown water dripped from the pipe, which turned into a trickle, then a stream and then a gush that gradually cleared as it splashed on the ground.

Everyone there gave a cheer, and the children immediately ran forward to jump and splash in the growing puddles. Morgan shook Etienne's hand, along with the two men who had assisted them. The women and children all crowded around the spurting hose, holding their hands out, letting the liquid splash over them.

"Remember, that water has to be filtered and purified before drinking, so try not to get any in your mouth." Kelleson's warnings were only partially heeded as the children splashed each other in the muddy puddles.

Morgan had extricated himself from the admiring pats and hugs from the joyous villagers, as well, and presently stood beside Kelleson with his arms folded. "Ah, let 'em have their fun—it's not often something like this comes along for them, I suppose."

She glanced up at him, her brow furrowed. "Spoken like someone who's never cared for a five-year-old with dysentery. All right, children, come away. Etienne, let's turn it off until you can get the containers for storage ready. And since Mr. Morgan here seems to be so handy—" she pinned him with another arched look "—perhaps he can help you with putting up that water tank you've been wanting to get done."

It was Morgan's turn to arch an eyebrow. "You been holding out on me, Etienne?"

The diminutive man smiled. "It's a project I've wanted to try for the past year, but I've just not been sure we could do it, and then the parts have been impossible to get and, well, I think you already know how it is here."

"Yeah, but now you've got something you didn't have before—me. Come on, let's take a look at what you've got. That is, if I'm not needed elsewhere for the moment?" Morgan glanced at Kelleson, who regarded him with an expression somewhere between admiration and annoyance.

"Yes, that would be fine." She turned on her heel and walked away, Morgan watching her the whole while.

I hate to see her leave, but I must confess I like watching her go, he thought with a rueful smile before heading off with Etienne.

**9**

Raised voices interrupted Hachtman as he was trying to compose a report of the group's progress and activities to email back to the company. With an irritated frown, he saved his document, rose from his stool and exited his tent. He stalked through the camp, brushing by men who knew to get out of his way when they saw the tall man walking with such purpose.

As soon as he reached the cluster of trucks, he took in the scene. Kapleron stood in the center of a half dozen of his security personnel, all of them looking as though they were going hunting for black caiman. Each carried a FAMAS bullpup assault rifle, with a bandoleer of magazines, sidearms, and one even toting a Milkor MGL-140 multibarrel automatic grenade launcher, capable of laying down devastating ordnance against lightly armored opponents.

"Exactly what is going on here?" Hachtman didn't have to raise his voice to make the activity around the trucks come to a stop—his presence alone did that.

Kapleron rammed a magazine into his FAMAS and yanked the cocking lever back. "One of them feckin' locals killed one of my boys last night. We're out t'get some payback—let 'em know they can't mess with us."

Hachtman heaved a sigh. "Give me the details."

"We had sensor reports of a few jaguars moving through

the southwest quadrant, so I sent out a team to capture some, nothin' unusual there."

Hachtman nodded. Kapleron had connections in Europe and Asia that would pay upward of six figures for live tropical animals—especially a jaguar. Hachtman had approved the side venture with strict instructions that it not impede their primary mission in the area. "Go on."

"They came back and said while they were chasin' one, Barent got surprised and taken out—cracked his skull, they did, and all without a sound. Wasn't any jungle cat that did that—not without taking a bite or two. So one of the locals must have gotten the drop on him. They need to be punished."

"And this fits in with your primary objective how?"

Kapleron swung around, and for a moment Hachtman actually thought the smaller man was about to point his assault rifle at him. "My men were only a mile from the main camp. If those bastards are comin' that close, they could stumble onto the place. Best for us to do them before they do us. You given any more thought to my suggestion from yesterday?"

"Yes, and I'm inclined to give you approval to carry it out, provided you can make it look like what you said—a warring faction killing the other village."

"No problem. Like I said, we can make it look like militia did it, or even those pansy natives. The message'll get across, and while they're tryin' t'figure out who killed who, they'll keep lookin' there and stay out of here."

Hachtman nodded again. "Just don't make any mistake that would lead them or the local military right to our doorstep."

Kapleron's voice dropped dangerously low. "Are you questioning my ability to carry out this mission, Mr. Hachtman?"

"Not at all, I just want you to achieve your mission objective and understand what your role is. We've got a job to carry out here. I don't want you embarking on missions of petty revenge. If, while completing your primary mission, you have a chance to satisfy your bloodlust against these savages, fine, but do not forget—" Hachtman stepped close to the smaller man, looming over him, despite the armament Kapleron held "—*never* forget who's paying you and your men to carry out our goals—and what Paracor will do to you if they aren't completed to our satisfaction."

Despite the fact that Hachtman wasn't armed, he had the satisfaction of seeing Kapleron swallow and drop his gaze first. "Right, *baas*. Don't you worry—we'll have those bastards spitted and gone before you can spit."

The overseer turned his head and did just that, sending a spray of saliva to the ground. "Then you and your men had better get moving, Mr. Kapleron."

**10**

Kelleson led Bolan to the north side of the village, to the goat pen, where Paul Wilberson waited for them.

Along with the water pump, the pen was one of her proudest achievements. She'd fought hard to expand the tiny herd from its meager three animals to the rambunctious dozen they had today, with the additional milk from the females a godsend for the growing children. Unfortunately, unlike the well, she feared that the goats might be in the most trouble, as several of them had come down with a strange disease, and she was in the middle of trying to diagnose and treat it. That was why she had put in the request for anyone with either veterinary or animal husbandry experience to visit.

She just hoped Wilberson knew what he was doing, as she watched the man examine the brown-and-white, round-bellied goats, all of which bleated and butted up against the tall man as he palpated one's jawline, humming softly to keep the animal calm. Kelleson was surprised to see how relaxed he looked while he worked. The tenseness in his body had eased, and the hint of a smile slowly curled one corner of his mouth. He checked the billy's teeth, then let the animal go to rejoin the rest of the herd.

"Well?" Kelleson hated the anxious tone in her voice.

Wilberson straightened and turned to her. "It's a problem, but nothing too serious. Your herd's got what's called *Caseous lymphadenitis,* caused by two bacteriums, *coryne* and *pseudotuberculosis*. Vets refer to it as 'cheesy gland' or 'yolk boils.' It's a fairly common infection, usually caused by abrasions in the goat's mouth or elsewhere on its head."

"It's not contagious for humans, is it?" Bolan asked.

"Good question, but no, we'll all be fine handling them. The best thing to do will be to give them something like Eweguard, which will not only take care of this, but also prevent five clostridial diseases—the long, scientific names of which I won't bore you with right now—and also control internal parasites, nasal bot and itch mite. A handy little drug, especially out here."

Kelleson smiled. "You sound like a commercial for the stuff."

Wilberson returned her grin. "Only because I know how well it works. Any decent farm-supply store should carry it. The only question is where the nearest decent store is."

Kelleson jerked her thumb toward the lone, rutted road out of town. "Back in the city, and a day's travel away. However, one of the other villages nearby had a similar problem, and they might still have some of that vaccine you mentioned, or something else that works just as well. Looks like I'll be taking the group on a field trip tomorrow. Want to come?"

"Sure, if we can finish trimming the goats' hooves by then," Wilberson said.

"What do you mean? I thought their feet were fine."

"Whoever's been caring for these guys hasn't quite got the correct ratio of toe to heel on the ground. They're also a bit overgrown, although nothing too bad yet. It's a fine point, but an important one, otherwise mud and dung can get in there and cause putrefaction and hoof rot, neither of which you want in your herd, of course. Since you don't have any rocks for the goats to walk on to condition their hooves, they grow faster, and require more frequent care."

"How long will it take?"

"One person doing a dozen goats, it's going to take a few hours."

"If you show me what to do, I can lend a hand, get it done faster," Bolan said.

"I'll help, as well," Kelleson said.

Wilberson frowned. "Don't you need to oversee the other volunteers?"

"Not really, a crew is helping them construct their hut for the next few days, so that'll keep them busy. How about it?"

"Okay. It's a handy skill to have, although you'll both need a bit of practice before you're ready to tackle one on your own. We'll need hoof shears, a small pick if you have it, a small brush—an old toothbrush would do—a bucket of water and a small carpenter's plane. Iodine, too. While you're getting all that together, I'll cull out the worst of the lot, and we'll do them first."

Bolan went to collect the necessary items, getting the plane from Etienne and the rest of the items from the women in the village. He returned with his arms laden with tools, along with two pairs of heavy cloth gloves. "I figured we'd need these, as well."

"Good call, thanks." Wilberson separated four goats from the rest of the herd, pulled the heavy gloves on, then knelt and stroked his first patient, a small kid who bleated nervously. He murmured soothing words until the goat calmed down enough to stand still. He bent its foreleg back and held out his hand to Kelleson. "Hand me the hoof pick."

She did so and watched as he cleaned the underside of accumulated detritus. Then Wilberson asked for the toothbrush and water, and washed the outside of the hoof.

"See these growth lines, running parallel with the hairline where the leg meets the hoof itself? That's the proper angle to trim each hoof parallel to, as the toe grows faster than the heel. Hand me the shears."

She did so and watched him work, trimming slices of hard hoof off with sure, deft movements. "Take a look—see how I've gotten past the white and down to the pink area? That's as far as you should go. Again, the toe and heel should be at the same angle as the nearest growth ring. Now I trim the other hoof." He set the one hoof down and cleaned then trimmed the other foreleg, then held both of them together, eliciting another bleat from the goat. "They don't like this as much." Holding both legs together in one hand, he used the carpenter's plane to level both feet.

Kelleson winced as she watched the plane rasp across the hooves. "Is that blood coming out? Doesn't that hurt them?"

"Not nearly as much as improperly trimmed hooves might. He'll be all right. But that's what the iodine is for, to prevent infection." Wilberson sprinkled a bit on the bottom of each hoof and set them down. "Now for the hind legs."

In another few minutes, the trimming was complete, and he released the kid, who took off to join his brothers and sisters on the far side of the pen. Wilberson stood and looked at Bolan. "Okay, want to give it a shot?"

"Let's do it." He knelt in the mud as Wilberson culled another goat from the herd, this one a white-furred doe with floppy ears. He grasped the foreleg firmly and bent it back until the mud- and dung-encrusted hoof was visible. "Not a pretty sight," Bolan said.

"Don't worry, you'll get used to it—I would advise breathing through your mouth as much as possible, however."

"Thanks, I don't think I'll have any trouble remembering that." Bolan breathed shallowly while cleaning the hoof bottom, then washed it before taking up the shears.

"Remember, you aren't hurting them. Trim through the white area until you reach the pink, and try to keep your cuts parallel to the nearest growth ring. Go slow at first, until you get the hang of it."

Cooper set the shears on the hoof as he'd seen Wilberson do, and squeezed the handles together, expecting the goat to squeal in pain. A thin curl of hoof sheared off and fell to the ground, but the goat didn't even seem to notice.

Letting out the breath she hadn't been aware she was holding, Kelleson watched Bolan cut twice more, then move to the other side, trimming that edge so that it was even with the first.

Wilberson nodded. "You're a natural. Okay, just a bit more off there, and you're ready for the other hoof, then we'll plane them even. Nancy, why don't you get in here and watch this, as well, then we'll switch on the next one."

Bolan did the same on the other foot, then Wilberson helped him hold them together. He let Bolan do most of the work, only stopping him by placing his hand in front of the plane. "All right, that's enough. Now for the hind legs."

They finished with the second goat and moved on to the next, working in tandem—Bolan holding each animal in place while Kelleson did the front hooves, then switching places with him to the back after the second goat nearly kicked her in the jaw when she'd tried to restrain it. When she was done with the back hooves, Bolan stopped her by placing his hand on hers over the carpenter's plane. "Any more and you might go too deep. Let's get some iodine on that."

Kelleson was quite surprised at how comfortable his touch was—a far cry from the major's roughness of the day before. In fact, it had been months since anyone had touched her like that. The natives were always very polite around her, but kept a respectful distance, which she encouraged. Shrugging off the sudden warm flush that spread through her, Kelleson concentrated on her work.

They were just moving on to their third one when Wilberson suddenly grimaced. "Uh—I gotta take a walk for a bit. You guys gonna be all right here until I return?"

"I think we can handle things until you get back, Paul," Kelleson said, trying not to sound too eager about being left alone with the journalist.

"Okay, I'll be back as soon as I can." He didn't so much walk as trot in the direction of the latrine.

Bolan watched him with a rueful grin. "Some folks just don't adjust to the food and water down here as fast as others."

"You certainly seem pretty comfortable here, Mr. Cooper."

"Call me Matt. I've been around here and there over the years. That's what I love about my job—it takes me to the most interesting places, and I get to meet the most interesting people."

It sounded like exactly what a globe-trotting journalist would say, and yet Kelleson sensed something hidden under his words, another meaning that she couldn't quite parse. "Well, we're grateful to have you here, Matt."

"Glad to be here, Ms. Kelleson."

"Nancy, please. You'll be here long enough that we might as well dispense with those kinds of formalities right away."

"Works for me."

Bolan didn't break the companionable silence until they took a break after trimming half the herd. "Nancy, I know this isn't any of my business, but about what happened yesterday—"

Kelleson held up her hand to forestall him. "Look, I appreciate you coming in when you did, but it wasn't anything I couldn't handle—really."

Bolan stared directly at her, and Kelleson got the feeling he saw right through her assumed bravado. The truth was that she hadn't known what she would have done if Medina had pressed his assault. The journalist's appearance had saved her from having to make that decision, but she hadn't slept well that night, her dreams haunted by dark violence.

He crossed his arms. "Perhaps you could have, but remember the dozen other guys with the automatic rifles standing around in the village while he paid his little visit? Remember what you said to me about the pride of these people yesterday? Well, I don't know about you, but I wouldn't want to injure the pride of a man who could order the slaughter of the entire population of this place with a wave of his hand if he wanted."

"I've been here long enough to know that Medina wouldn't do that to these people—he couldn't afford that kind of attention." But even as she said it, a voice in her head nagged her, whispering, *Are you sure about that?* The fact was, the big American might have been right. Showing Medina up in front of his own men might have given him the excuse to take out his embarrassment and anger on the villagers.

"You've been here long enough to ingratiate yourself to the villagers, and I'm sure they're grateful for the things and assistance you've given them. To the military, however—especially the likes of Medina—you're one of two things, either a potential witness to any trouble he might be involved in, or a focal point to rally the village itself against him if necessary. Either one makes you a target." Bolan dropped his penetrating gaze and looked at the ground. "Also, well, it sounded like Medina was trying to, I don't know, blackmail you or something."

Kelleson pulled away from him. "Just how long were you standing outside my hut?"

The journalist held up his hands. "Hold on now, I just heard him mention something about 'your time here would be at an end sooner.' Or something like that. But come on, when I saw you two in there it didn't look like any kind of normal conversation—it looked like he was trying to extort something out of you."

"Do you always jump to such wild conclusions on such little evidence?" Kelleson shook her head in disbelief. "Come on, we have to get the rest of the herd finished before nightfall."

"Nancy, I know what I saw—"

"And I told you to forget it, Matt. If anything, it was a misunderstanding by both you and the major, and I'll thank you to drop the subject, all right? Let's get back to work." She walked over and selected one of the goats they hadn't worked on yet, guiding it over to him. "Ready?"

Without a word, he bent over the animal and starting trimming. Kelleson alternated glances between him and the goat underneath her and knew this conversation probably wasn't over yet, as much as she wanted it to be.

Working diligently, she kept her gaze on the goat hooves, avoiding her partner's eyes as much as possible. When Wilberson returned, he didn't comment on the silence, but began working on another goat.

The three continued this way until a shout from the other side of the village raised all of their heads. Seconds later, Etienne came running toward them.

"Nancy, come quick. A boy from the next village just came into town, looking half-dead!"

## 11

"We're ready for you, Mr. Hachtman."

Hachtman took the offered headset with its attached microphone from the mercs' communications man and slipped it on, adjusting it on his oblong head. "Testing, testing, one, two. Mr. Kapleron, can you hear me?"

"Yeah, and that better be all I hear from you till we're finished, understand?"

"Unless I feel the situation warrants it, I will leave the execution of this mission entirely in your hands. On the ground, you are in charge."

Over the security leader's objections, Hachtman had ordered him wired for video and sound, saying he wanted to keep an eye on the mission as it unfolded. Kapleron had grumbled about the idea, but as Hachtman had suspected, he went along when he saw there was no getting around the orders. The businessman hadn't even had to wave his big stick of a bad performance review affecting the man's bonus—he knew the South African's bloodlust would outweigh any protest he might have—and had simply waited him out.

He watched as the squad of ten armed men drove through the jungle, their vehicles' headlights barely illuminating a few yards through the foggy jungle. The village they had picked for their test was ten miles away, and as soon as

Kapleron had been given the go sign, he'd selected his men and they'd set out for their target within the hour.

Although the distance wasn't that great, the condition of the road varied from passable to almost impossible, and even the tough four-wheel-drive Range Rovers had their work cut out for them on some of the more washed-out sections. Twice the men had needed to get out and winch one of the SUVs free from the axle-deep mud bogging it down. The trip had taken just over two hours—about as long as Hachtman had estimated. But once they'd finally reached the outskirts of the village, Kapleron pulled both Rovers to the side of the dirt road and cut the engine. After making sure his team was ready to go—including distributing the carved wooden spears that would be used to disguise their assault—he led them into the rainforest toward the village.

Hachtman made sure the digital recorders, a primary and two backups, were all running perfectly, then turned his attention back to the over-the-shoulder view he had of the men as they cut their trail, as if he was walking right beside them.

After a few minutes of quick, silent movement, broken only by the rhythmic rise and fall of the men's machetes, Kapleron held up a fisted hand. All of the men stopped immediately. He pointed at one man with a hard rifle case over his shoulder, then pointed into the canopy. The man trotted to a suitable tree, attached something to his combat boots and scrambled up the branchless trunk like a monkey.

When he reached a suitable height, he leaned back. Hachtman saw spikes on the bottom of his boots digging into the trunk. Reaching behind his head, the man took out what looked like a small seat with nylon straps attached to each end. Looping the strap around the tree, he cinched it tight, the seat resting at a ninety-degree angle to the trunk. The man tested it carefully, holding on to the tree in case the seat failed, then put all his weight on it. When it held, he uncased his rifle, affixed a long silencer on the end of the barrel, uncapped his scope and turned it on, then made one final adjustment to his position and gave the men on the ground a thumbs-up.

Kapleron signaled the rest of his men forward. They traveled about thirty yards before the target village could be seen—just as the daily rain began to fall. "Right on feckin' time," Hachtman heard Kapleron mutter.

There was no movement around the scattered huts. The rain intensified, soaking the motionless men, but Kapleron and his men didn't seem bothered in the least. The quartet of killers just hunkered down a few yards from the clearing and watched.

"What the devil are they waiting for?" Hachtman asked under his breath, making sure the mute on his microphone was engaged.

The comm man monitoring the recordings, a hardened youth of twenty-six, blinked in confusion. "They're taking stock of the situation, making sure there are no surprises when they make their move. Standard operating procedure."

"But there's no one there now. They could be in and out in just a few minutes."

The merc leaned back and stared at Hachtman. "I am sure Mr. Kapleron knows exactly what he is doing…sir."

"Hmm, yes, I suppose so." Hachtman also waited. Five minutes passed. "That rain isn't going to last forever."

"Do not worry—he'll move when he is ready."

Hachtman didn't move a muscle, waiting for the signal to be given by the chief of security.

Finally, with a simple flick of his hand, Kapleron signaled his men to take their positions. Three pairs of men fanned out, two going left, one going right to flank. Kapleron and another man waited until the first pair were both ready to cover, then the two men moved into the village square, staying low, silenced pistols out and held at their sides.

Like most villages fortunate enough to have one, the water tank was off to one side, near the jungle, mounted on a framework of poles. Kapleron had designated it as the launch and meeting point for the men handling the operation. The two men leapfrogged through the village, one man advancing while the other covered him, and reached the tower without incident. Kapleron stood guard, glancing around the village perimeter, watching for any potential trouble.

It came in the form of two people slipping out of separate huts at the far end of the village. A young man and woman, giggling to each another, snuck through the silent clusters of homes, holding hands as they flitted from shadow to shadow.

The squad froze. Hachtman listened to the conversation between them.

"Leader, I have visual on both approaching targets. Permission to fire?"

"Negative, keep them covered, but let them approach. We'll take them out if necessary. All teams, hold your positions—do not move except on my order." Kapleron melted into the jungle, holding his pistol in front of him with both hands as he disappeared into the thick foliage.

The couple drew closer, and Hachtman saw that it was a native man and woman. They both took shelter under the tower, and the man tilted the woman's head up for a long kiss, his hand stealing down to cup her breast. She moaned and pressed her body against his, her mouth opening to him as he leaned against a strut.

Lost in each other, they didn't notice Kapleron slowly stand, aim his silenced pistol and fire two carefully placed shots, one into the head of each. The couple, still locked in each other's arms, collapsed to the ground. Kapleron strode over and put one more bullet into each unmoving form.

"They're down. I'll remove the bodies. Left, Right, Longshot, keep your eyes open for others and sing out the moment you see anyone."

As Kapleron hoisted the woman's body over his shoulder, the faint whine of a small cordless drill could be heard in the background. He walked a dozen yards into the underbrush to dump the limp form, hacking a few fronds to cover her before going back for the other one.

Waiting for the cry of alarm that could come at any

moment, Hachtman scarcely remembered to breathe while Kapleron picked up the other body and hauled it into the brush. When he was done, he signaled his partner to move left while he circled the village perimeter, joining up with their man on the left flank.

"Right Flank, are you in position and ready?" the South African merc asked.

"Affirmative."

"Rear Team, are you in position and ready?"

"Affirmative."

"Longshot, are you in position and ready?"

"Affirmative."

"Remember, everyone, no head shots, to the chest only. Execute."

With that Kapleron and his teammate moved to the nearest hut, a large, tent-shaped affair made of woven palm fronds. Leaning a pair of their spears against the wall near the door, the second man took up a position on the far side and waited until his leader gave the signal. Kapleron raised his silenced pistol and nodded.

The other man burst in through the door, tracking the nearest villager over the sights of his gun and firing. Kapleron was right behind him, catching the family by surprise and putting three of them down with shots to the chest before anyone else could move. Screams and shouts came from men, women and children as they tried to escape the brutal killers in their midst. Their efforts were in vain, for the two gunmen swept through the room in an efficient process, tracking down each and every person. One of them tried to escape by squirming through the frond wall, but no sooner had he gotten out then his body jerked and went still.

"This is Longshot, I have movement from middle huts. Am commencing fire on outside targets."

"Copy that, Longshot. Good hunting." Kapleron took a second to reload, then checked with each team. The rear team was taking out anyone that tried to flee into the jungle. When their sniper had taken out all targets outside, Kapleron and his partner continued their sweep through the village, dispensing death with each whispered shot from their pistols.

A few minutes later the main deed was done. Kapleron assembled his men on the ground and dispatched them to a hut, taking the spears with them. As they stepped inside, Hachtman realized what they were about to do and turned away as the spear points began stabbing into cooling flesh. His stomach churned as he watched Kapleron and his partner hide all evidence of their merciless assault on the village.

When they were all finished, the two-man teams retraced their steps to their leader, who led them all to their sniper's position and waited for him to disassemble and stow his weapon and gear, and climb down. The five men disappeared into the foliage, heading back to the Range Rovers.

"Mission accomplished, Doctor." Kapleron must have switched off the camera on his shoulder, for that monitor went dark right afterward.

Hachtman straightened, easing his kinked back muscles and aware of two urgent matters that needed attention—his full bladder and the strong possibility that he might vomit after seeing the slaughter so casually carried out in front of him.

"Make sure I have a copy of that video file," he said to the communications tech as he trotted out of the tent toward the latrine.

## 12

Bolan led the rush toward the large group of villagers at the other end of the village, with Kelleson, Wilberson, Morgan and Etienne all close behind. They came across the trio of college students clustered around a skinny boy of about twelve years old. Thomas Bonell had just picked him up and was carrying him toward the nearest hut.

"No, take him to mine," Kelleson said, pointing Bonell toward her hut, which had a corrugated metal roof. He headed for it, with her at his side.

Inside, she had Bonell lay the child on her bed and knelt beside him. "Everyone else out."

"All right, you all heard the lady." Bolan herded the rest of the volunteers toward the door.

"That means you, too, Cooper." She didn't look up as she checked the boy's pulse. The child stared at her with wide eyes, not moving a muscle. His arms and legs were covered in scrapes, insect bites and shallow cuts.

"Not a chance—you may need me."

"You've got paramedic training?"

"Close enough for here—you pick up a lot of survival skills in Third World countries."

"All right, his pulse is erratic and thready, and his breathing is rapid and shallow. What's that suggest to you?"

"That he's in shock. We should keep him warm and try to get him to eat something." Bolan felt the boy's forehead, then touched his hand. "He doesn't seem dehydrated, so an IV shouldn't be necessary." He pulled a brightly colored blanket over the boy's legs and stomach. "I don't suppose you know who he is or where he came from?"

"No, but I know who can find out." She went to the door and asked for Etienne. "Also, have the women heat any broth or stew we've got right away."

Etienne appeared in the doorway, and Kelleson waved him forward. "If you can, ask him who he is and where he came from."

The small man knelt by the boy's side and began talking to him in the Huaorani language. The boy just stared at him at first, but Etienne was patient and kept at it, eventually eliciting single words out of him.

"He says his name is Galo. He is from the village that is about thirty miles from here to the northwest. That is all I've learned so far."

Bolan and Kelleson stayed out of the man's way and watched. When a bowl of broth with chunks of tender pork and hominy swimming in it was brought in, Kelleson turned away to add the contents of a capsule to it, before slowly handing it to Etienne, who offered it to the boy.

Bolan, Kelleson and Etienne all remained silent as the boy reached for the bowl with trembling fingers and began to eat, picking chunks of meat out with his fingers. When he was finished, Etienne continued his questions, starting a dialogue with the boy that ran for a few minutes. When they were finished, Etienne pulled the blanket up and patted the boy on the head, talking briefly to him again before his eyes drooped closed and he fell asleep.

Etienne took them to the other side of the hut. "He is a very brave boy."

"Yes, but what happened to him? Where are his parents?" Kelleson asked.

"Apparently, about two days ago, a large truck came to their village. Men in 'green clothes'—his words—got out and began shooting everyone in the village—men, women,

children, everybody. He had been playing in the forest and
followed the truck back. He saw the whole thing. He lay in
the brush for an entire day and night, until he was sure they
weren't coming back, then set out to find help. He ended up
here."

"Do you know exactly where his village is?" Bolan asked.

"Yes, although it isn't easy to reach from here. It is a jour-
ney of several hours."

"Then we'd better get going as soon as possible," Bolan
replied.

BRACING HERSELF AGAINST the dashboard, Kelleson peered
through the windshield as Etienne wrestled with the Range
Rover's steering wheel, narrowly missing a tree by the side
of the narrow, muddy, single-lane road. The SUV brushed
against the trunk with a scrape of metal, but no harm done.

"Too close," he said, and Kelleson agreed with a nod.

From the rear passenger compartment, she heard a muttered "I could drive better than this blindfolded." Shooting
a venomous look at the speaker, she made Morgan suddenly
take an intense interest in the passing vegetation. Next to
him, Bolan rolled his eyes and grinned at Kelleson, making
her almost unable to resist returning his smile. Behind them,
she saw the second SUV, containing the rest of the SARE
volunteers, slip past the tree without difficulty, and she
glanced sidelong at Etienne, who had been working particularly hard ever since his return to the village, and noticed the
dark pouches under his eyes for the first time.

"Etienne, please slow down—the village will still be there
when we arrive."

The wiry man grunted. "We're almost there and only got
stuck once."

"Well, I don't want to be stuck at the other village with vehicle trouble, either. If we're going to make it back by nightfall, we need to get there, assess the situation and start back
quickly."

From the back Bolan said, "I hate to say it, but from what

the boy said, it sounds like we don't need to be in that much of a hurry."

Kelleson turned her glare on him. "That's a damn cold thing to say."

"Look, down here—like anywhere else where power comes mostly out of the barrel of a gun—there's always a risk of something like this happening." Bolan shot a glance at Morgan. "Right now we'd be better served putting our heads together to try to figure out who would gain by wiping out an entire village."

Morgan had turned from his examination of the forest and joined in the conversation. "Of course. What about your buddy, Major Medina—"

Kelleson twisted around to regard him, her eyes blazing. "Get this straight, 'cause I'm only going to say it once— Major Medina is *not* my friend in any way, shape or capacity."

Bolan held up his hands. "Whoa, I'm sure Elliot didn't mean it *that* way—you were being sarcastic, right?"

"Absolutely—sorry for the misunderstanding, Nancy. But my point is still valid—do you think he might have done this as a warning to other tribes in the area?"

"Look, I know the major is an opportunistic, sexist pig, however, he has actually done some good for the region. He took out an ultraviolent splinter cell of FARC back in January that was doing sweeps and taking children and young men to indoctrinate them into the rebel organization. I know he comes across as a man who's out for himself, but I don't see any way he would commit a cold-blooded act of genocide like this on his own."

"So does that mean Colombia's trying to stir up trouble on its border with Ecuador to start a war?" Bolan shook his head. "It doesn't make sense. They've got enough troubles internally with the drug trade to risk bloodying this country's nose and risking Chavez lending Ecuador aid against them in any kind of conflict. I can't see how the gain would be worth the risk."

"Hey, we're coming up to the village…" Etienne's voice trailed off as the Range Rover left the jungle and entered the outskirts of the community. Looking around, Kelleson felt a prickle of unease shiver down her spine.

Instead of the groups of vibrant men, women and children that should have been everywhere, the entire place was eerily still, with not a soul moving anywhere.

"What happened here?" Kelleson asked, then gasped as she spotted several motionless forms sprawled on the ground in the main square and near the huts, swarms of flies buzzing around them in the late afternoon heat. "Oh, my God."

The SUV hadn't even braked to a stop before Bolan and Morgan both jumped out, each saying the same thing. "Keep everyone inside the vehicles for—now—" They both looked at each other in brief confusion, and Kelleson seized her digital camera and the opportunity.

"Etienne, tell the others to stay put. I'm going to check this out," she said.

"Nancy, wait—it might be dangerous—" Bolan didn't get any further.

"Every day I spend here is dangerous. If the military did this, then I want proof. I want to see and record it with my own eyes. You two can come with, you can both help all you want, but you're not stopping me."

Bolan exchanged a glance with Morgan that carried an entire silent conversation between them, then he turned to her. "All right, but the three of us stick together until the village is cleared, and if we see anything nasty, we hightail it out of here. In fact, Etienne, get both SUVs turned around in case we need to get out of here in a hurry."

Morgan's eyes hadn't left the village as Bolan spoke, and then he chimed in. "The fact that nobody's shooting at us so far indicates that whatever did happen here, we missed it. But that doesn't mean someone isn't waiting to ambush us once we're deeper inside. Let's take a careful look around and go from there."

Opening her door, Kelleson slid out of her seat, camera in

hand, swallowing as she steeled herself for what they were about to see. Bolan stood behind her, and he moved up to walk next to her as they headed into the village. Behind her, Kelleson heard the Range Rovers as Etienne and the other driver turned them around. Other than that, the entire area was completely silent, with not even the local birds sounding their customary chorus of chirps and caws from the jungle. It was as if something had swept through the entire place and taken all life with it, leaving only an empty shell behind. Over the sweet-sour tang of wet, rotting vegetation, Nancy smelled the rich copper scent of spilled blood—and lots of it—overlaid with the gamy scent of spoiling meat.

"You going to be all right?" Bolan asked, seeing her swallow and raise a hand to her nose and mouth as they walked deeper into the village. He kept his hand near his back and the SIG Sauer concealed under his shirt. Morgan walked on their left, about three paces away—far enough to not be caught with them in case of an ambush, but close enough to assist immediately if needed.

She shook her head. "I'll be fine. Let's get this over with."

Kelleson and the two men approached the nearest body, a middle-aged man lying on his stomach, unmoving. Bolan and Morgan walked to the left and the right of the prone body, each man searching the jungle for signs of life. Kelleson cautiously approached the corpse.

"Don't touch him." Bolan grabbed her arm, but Kelleson shook him off.

"I know, I know, but I want to roll him over—it looks like he was injured, and I want to see how." Looking around, she spotted a long stick, its end caked with what looked like dried blood and hair. Steadying her roiling stomach, she reached for it and used the clean end to lever the body over, recoiling in horror at what she saw.

"Oh, good heavens…"

The man's face had been severely beaten, his features a swollen, bloody ruin. Kelleson dropped the stick and backed away, clapping her hands to her mouth. She stumbled around the side of a hut, and Bolan soon heard the sounds of her being violently ill.

Morgan had moved up to Bolan's side. "This didn't kill him," he said, pointing at the man's chest, where a trio of bloody holes marked bullet wounds. "Looks like someone shot him, then beat his face in."

A rustling could be heard from the hut a few yards away, and both Bolan and Morgan tensed, their eyes flicking to each other. Bolan nodded at it, and they approached, Morgan taking the right, Bolan the left. He picked up the bloody pole as they came upon the dark hole of the hut entrance. The reek of rotting meat was almost overpowering, even to Bolan, who'd seen death and carnage around the world.

The rustling was heard again, along with a strange tearing sound. When he was sure Morgan was ready, Bolan stepped inside the hut, pole at the ready.

A loud, ragged squawk came from the lone inhabitant of the hut—a large black vulture in the middle of dining on one of the several dead bodies inside. Thrusting the pole at the scavenger, Bolan drove the bird off the body and out of the hut, the animal squawking indignantly the entire way.

"Damn—these people never had a chance." Morgan squatted next to a woman slumped against the wall, her once-colorful T-shirt caked in thick, dried blood.

A noise from the hut made both men turn to see Kelleson in the doorway, watching as they prowled the area, exchanging those silent glances again. "Why? Why would anyone do this to a harmless village?"

"There's plenty of reasons." His right hand still tucked behind his back, Bolan approached another body, this one with its skull shattered, brain matter leaking out in a dark pool that had been absorbed by the ground. "A lot of people find it easier to eliminate an indigenous population than to relocate them. In a few months, this place would be overgrown with vegetation, and no one would even know anybody had existed here. Then it would be time for the new inhabitants to move in."

"What? You can't be serious."

"No, he may be right, Nancy." Morgan pointed to the bodies. "The signs everywhere point to an assault from a disciplined outside force. Other than the occasional physical violence against a victim, everyone has been killed by large-caliber firearms—which is definitely the military's style, whose men also carry assault rifles."

"But that doesn't make any sense—" Kelleson was interrupted by a shout from outside.

"Hey! What's going on over there?"

Someone had rolled down the window of the second SUV, and one of the college students—Bonell, Bolan thought—had his head stuck out the window and was calling to them. His innocent comment brought glares from both Bolan and Morgan, both of whom waved their palms toward the ground in the universal "keep quiet" motion.

"Keep it down!" Bolan stressed.

"Fucking amateurs." Morgan shook his head. "Nancy, why don't you fill in the Hardy Boys, and Cooper and I will take a look inside the rest of the huts."

"Right." She turned and stalked toward the second SUV, intending to dress down the young man.

The moment she was out of earshot, Morgan turned to Bolan. "If you're a freelance journalist, I'm the friggin' President."

"Well, Mr. President, if you want to continue our sweep, you can go first into the next hut we check."

"That wasn't what I meant, Cooper, and you know it."

Bolan stepped close to the other man, pitching his voice low. "Right now it doesn't matter who I am. What matters is that we have American citizens right in the middle of what looks like the planned eradication of this native population. I think the one thing we can both agree on at the moment is that we don't want them to get caught in the cross fire, correct?"

"Yeah, but I don't need to divide my time watching for whoever's doing this *and* keeping an eye on my back at the same time. For all we know, you could be a plant from whoever's running around slaughtering these people."

"So could you." Bolan pointed out.

"I could, but I fucking know I'm not. I can't say the same about you." Morgan looked as though he was about to take a swing at Bolan, who narrowed his eyebrows.

"Elliot, I can assure you—although I cannot prove it—that you and I are on the same side here. Let's finish our sweep and then decide the next step, all right?"

Before Morgan could answer, a commotion near the SUVs made both men's heads turn. Kelleson was coming back to them, followed by the two college students, who pulled up abruptly as the smell from the bodies hit them.

Before they got too close, Morgan snapped, "All right, let's get this done. But when we get back to camp, you and I are gonna have a long talk about what's going on here."

"I look forward to it," Bolan replied.

"For the last time, I told you guys to stay back there. And what the hell's going on here?" Kelleson actually stepped between the two men. "All right, both of you calm down. Morgan, Cooper, we need to check the rest of these huts, in case anyone is still alive inside. Everyone else, get back inside the SUV, and *stay there* this time, got it?"

Bonell and Mike Saderson both grumbled their assent. "What the hell's going on here?" Bonell asked.

Kelleson was about to answer, but Bolan beat her to it. "It seems that the villagers have been attacked by some unknown party that killed practically all of them. For now, I'd suggest doing what Nancy says and staying there. If you see anything unusual, yell for us, and we'll come running. Above all, do not leave the vehicle, or investigate *any* unusual occurrence around here yourself, understand?"

"You got it, man." The students beat feet back to the SUVs.

"Tell Etienne we're checking out the rest of the place." Kelleson took a deep breath and turned back to face the silent village again. "We'll be back in a few minutes."

## 13

Kelleson, Morgan and Bolan headed back into the deathly silent village, ready to finish their hut-to-hut sweep.

Morgan and Bolan were still exchanging wary glances, and Kelleson, apparently having had enough, whirled to catch both of them doing it again. "Look, do you two need to go behind a tree or a rock or something and beat each other's brains out until only one of you's left standing? Because I don't need this bullshit sniping right now—there are bigger problems to solve than soothing either of your bruised egos. Now, anyone who can't play nice can wait for me back at the Range Rovers. I don't have time to babysit two macho assholes who can't control their base impulses. Are we clear?"

The two men glared at each other one last time, then both nodded.

"All right, let's go." Kelleson walked to the first hut, the spoiled smell of death already wafting from it, and reached for the blanket covering the door, but was stopped by Bolan.

"On the off chance anyone might be waiting inside, let's not give them a perfect target silhouetted by the sun, okay?"

"Right." Kelleson flushed, embarrassed that she had forgotten such an elementary rule. "Although I'd have thought anyone wanting to shoot us would have had ample opportunity already. How do you want to do this?"

"No offense, but why don't Elliot and I do the initial

survey, and you watch our back, in case someone tries to ambush us from the jungle."

Kelleson readied her camera. "Fair enough."

The two men approached the doorway without a sound, Morgan on the left, Bolan on the right. Once they were both in position, Bolan nodded at Morgan, who reached over and yanked the blanket off the wooden pole holding it up. The two men disappeared into the blackness of the hut's interior, while Kelleson craned her neck, trying to see inside. After a few seconds—the hut was only about twelve feet across—they both sounded off.

"Clear left."

"Clear right, as well." A moment later they exited the thatched-roof building, their faces ashen.

"I'm going in." Kelleson strode toward the door, but was stopped by Cooper's hand on her shoulder.

"Nancy, I don't think you should go in there—"

"The hell I'm not." She held up the camera. "This has to be documented."

Morgan looked up from where he leaned against the hut wall, hands on his knees. "It's her stomach, let her go if she wants to see it that badly."

"And as you saw, I already emptied it at the first hut. I'll be all right." Brushing by the tall man, Kelleson stepped inside the dim building.

The stench alone made her stomach clench and her bowels tighten as if someone had just kicked her between the legs. The walls of the hut were so dark that at first she thought the family that had lived here had painted them, but upon closer inspection, she realized that the thick liquid smeared and spattered on the walls was clotting, drying blood.

Kelleson fought to control her gorge while her eyes adjusted to the dimness. The interior was a shambles, with shattered handmade wooden furniture everywhere, including the remnants of a table sticking out of the back wall. Looking down before she stepped in any farther, she froze as she realized that she had almost stepped on the small, motionless arm of a child, a girl, maybe nine or ten years old, cut almost into two pieces while she tried to run away from whoever had burst in to slaughter her family. She was only a step away from the doorway, from the outside, sun and life. Her arms were twisted in the dirt, her legs bent as if she had tried to keep moving even after she had been chopped to the floor. Blood had coagulated on her shoulders, arms and back, coating her in a thick, red-black layer of sticky wetness as it had spurted out to stain her skin and the hard-packed ground.

Kelleson tore her gaze away from the small body, but wherever she looked, her eyes took in more death. The body of a woman lay half in a hammock, her dangling arms and legs, still dripping blood, already attracting army ants, which swarmed around her limbs, climbing onto her in rows. She'd been shot at close range, the bullets pulping her head so severely that the pale yellow remains of her splintered skull could be seen amid her ruined scalp and face, one ear dangling by a strip of skin.

But the worst was yet to come. In a corner of the hut was another hammock with a pile of blankets on it, the middle of them dark and sopping wet. Kelleson took a step closer, then another. With a trembling hand, she reached for a corner of the blanket and pulled it back, letting out a long, shuddering breath as she saw what was underneath.

In the middle of the slung canvas was an even smaller child, maybe four years old, still clutching a handmade woven doll to her breast. Her killer had shot her through the heart, leaving a small pool of blood to drip onto the floor underneath the hammock. There seemed to be no sign of the father, giving Kelleson a good picture of what had happened.

He was killed outside in the initial burst of fire, then these killers burst inside to slaughter his family, she thought.

Breathing through her mouth and trying to keep her hands steady, she took a dozen shots of the interior and the bodies. The camera's bright flash threw the carnage into stark relief, illustrating every cut, every wound and the doomed bodies, frozen in their last, terrified moments. Kelleson's stomach churned every time she pressed the button.

At last, knowing there was nothing more she could do, Kelleson made for the doorway on unsteady legs. The hot sunlight had never seemed more welcoming. Away from the charnel-house smell, she took several deep breaths to clear her nose and lungs, although a part of her knew she would never forget that thick, sickly sweet odor.

"You gonna be all right?" Bolan walked over to her, but she waved him off.

"I don't know if I'll ever be all right again." She hawked up saliva and spit in the dust. Without a word, Bolan handed her a bottle of water, which she used to rinse her mouth and spit again. Wiping her lips with the back of her hand, Kelleson handed the bottle back and headed for the next hut. "Come on. Let's finish this."

The two men fell in behind her, and they went through the curved row of huts surrounding the main square. Inside every building, they found more atrocities, men and women killed in horrific ways, from elderly people with their heads smashed apart by bullets to one young man who had been shot, then impaled on a spear that had stuck him to the wall of the hut, where he had died trying to pull the slick shaft from his body.

Kelleson took pictures of everything, stopping only once, when she came across a brother and sister, each no more than five, who had died in each other's arms. She had taken a moment to step outside and throw up again, then calmly returned and kept taking pictures.

"Jesus Christ, who'd do such a thing?" Morgan asked. "This is worse than some of the places I've been where they knew how to torture, believe me."

Bolan shook his head. "I don't know—and where are the survivors? Other than Galo, we haven't seen any evidence of anyone else alive. But its unlikely the team, no matter how well trained, could have killed each and *everyone* here— that's just too neat."

"We can bat around theories about who's behind this all night long later. Right now, I just want to finish the job. We've got two more to go, then we can get the hell out of here and radio for some kind of help." Steeling herself, Kelleson was about to sweep the blanket aside when she heard a noise from inside. She froze, straining her ears to try to catch it again.

"Nancy, what's the hold—" Morgan began before she cut him off with a raised hand.

"Shh! I heard something inside," she whispered. "Go to the other side."

Morgan crept to the right side of the door, his right hand tucked behind his back again. Kelleson felt Bolan's presence behind her, solid and formidable.

"Sure you don't want me to take point?" he whispered.

She shook her head, wiping away the sweat that had suddenly appeared from her forehead with the back of her hand. "No, I'm fine. Cooper, on three, you right, me left."

He nodded, and she reached for the blanket, ripping it away and lunging into the hut, ready to punch or tackle whoever might come at her.

The interior of this hut was cleaner than most, with light coming in from a window on the east wall. Kelleson saw a crumpled body in the corner, but her attention was immediately drawn to the young boy in the center of the room, holding a bloodstained machete, his wide eyes white against his tan skin. Unlike the others, he was unmarked by the slaughter that had swept through his village.

For a moment, the two stared at each other, the child holding the dripping blade in front of him, Kelleson with her arms out, palms held up, not daring to move. She was sure he wouldn't be able to hurt her before she could disarm him, but was more concerned that one of the men might do something rash when they saw the weapon.

"Nancy?" Bolan's voice broke the stillness. The boy started and shifted the machete toward him.

Kelleson watched him out of the corner of her eye, the

muscular man already tensed to pounce. "Don't move, Cooper. Don't make another sound." She returned her concentration on the boy, smiling in what she hoped was a calming gesture. "Hello," she said in his native tongue. "Where are your parents?"

"Dead...all dead...I hide in here...away from the screaming...everyone was screaming." The boy's arms trembled as the words tumbled out. While he talked, Kelleson edged closer, trying to gauge the distance between her and the machete. The boy shook himself out of his stupor and clenched the hilt of the large knife tighter, raising it to ward her off.

"I can get him from the side—just keep his attention—"

"No, don't do a goddamn thing!" Kelleson ordered out of the side of her mouth. "I need to establish rapport, otherwise he'll never talk to us. Just give me a minute."

She stared at the boy, trying to catch his gaze with her own. "What's your name?"

"Nampa."

"My name is Nancy, Nampa, and it's very nice to meet you. Can you do me a favor and put that machete down?"

"No!" The bloody blade danced in the air. "No, you'll kill me like you did everyone else!"

"No, Nampa, I won't, I promise. Look, I don't even have a machete. I don't have any kind of weapon, see?" Kelleson slowly turned around, risking the boy attacking her while her back was turned, but knowing that Bolan would intercept him before he could get that far. "See? I'm not carrying anything that could hurt you."

His face twisted in confusion, and the blade wavered a bit. Kelleson pressed her advantage. "I want to take you away from all of this, to keep you safe from the people that killed the rest of your family and friends."

"So much screaming...but they just kept shooting everyone!" The boy looked at the machete as if he'd never seen it before, the gore-slicked weapon dropping from his hands as he started to cry.

Kelleson walked over to him and enfolded the sobbing boy

in her arms. "It's all right. It's going to be all right. You're safe now." Even as she mouthed the platitudes, she knew his life would never be the same again. She picked him up, the boy's skinny arms wrapping around her neck and clinging to her. Turning to Bolan, she nodded toward the door. "Let's go."

Outside, Morgan's eyes widened in surprise at Kelleson's load. "Found one alive, huh?"

She nodded. "Yeah. Come on, let's get out of here. I've seen enough death for today—not to mention the rest of my life."

**14**

Bolan was very quiet during the rocking, jouncing ride back to their village.

He'd seen a lot of horrors during his endless war on terror, both witnessing and dealing out his share of death, and thought he'd gotten used to the savagery man could inflict on his fellows. But the destruction he'd just seen—men and women killed just because of where they lived—made most everything else pale in comparison. Even wanton killing generally served some kind of purpose—terrorism, looting, conquering of a people or territory. But the bodies he'd seen strewed around like so much human cordwood didn't resemble victims of any of that—just, according to their killers, vermin that had to be exterminated.

That familiar fire was burning in the pit of his stomach—the desire to track down those responsible for this callous slaughter and exterminate them. The biggest problem was that he was at least two hours away from being able to report in to Stony Man Farm unseen. And every minute lost meant the trail of whoever had wiped out that village grew colder.

Kelleson had herded everyone out of the village immediately after their sweep, over Morgan's public protests and Bolan's private ones. Morgan had still pushed to stay, but she'd overruled him, saying that they needed to get back to the village and report this to the proper authorities.

And that was exactly what she was trying to do. In the front passenger seat, Kelleson kept trying to raise Major Medina, but only heard static every time she released the mike's transmit button. "Damn it!" She slammed the mike down on the dashboard. Huddled on her lap, Nampa whimpered and shied away from her. "Sorry, sorry, it's all right, I didn't mean to get upset." Etienne slumped in the driver's seat, completely silent, driving back with exaggerated care.

Watching Morgan out of the corner of his eye, Bolan was somewhat gratified to see that the scene at the village had apparently affected him, as well. He stared out the window, also apparently not in the mood for conversation. Works for me, he thought.

The thigh pocket of his cargo pants shook slightly, and he looked down to see the cloth shake again. His sat phone was receiving a call or text message. Glancing up to make sure everyone else was distracted with their own thoughts, Bolan slid his hand inside and pulled the small phone out. The small screen had turned red, indicating a high-level text message had been received. Keeping the phone hidden between his leg and the door, Bolan read it.

TS/eyes only

Elliot Morgan is security operative with Sulexco surveying. Could be useful source of info. Approach him and pool all available information.

Files attached for Nancy Kelleson and Major Andrés Medina.

Good luck.

SMF.

There was a sat phone number for Morgan included. Bolan's eyes flicked over the other passengers. No one had taken any interest in his actions. He saved the attached files for later review, then typed a quick shorthand reply with his thumb.

Striker to SMF

Nearby village wiped out by unknown hostiles—see attached pics. Found 2 survivors—will try to find cause. Scan for any unknown camps within a 100-klick radius of both villages. Will report in again as soon as I have more info.

He attached the pictures and short video he had taken while clearing the village, then sent the whole package to headquarters. Bolan was determined to find out who was responsible for this travesty, and Stony Man Farm's resources would be invaluable in doing this.

Closing the phone, he returned it to his pocket and turned his attention to Kelleson in the front seat. Leaning forward, he made sure she noticed him before speaking, so he wouldn't startle her. "How's the little guy doing?"

"He fell asleep once he calmed down, but he's still skittish."

"Worried about him slipping into shock?"

"I'm keeping an eye on his vitals, which seem strong, and he's not feverish or disoriented, so I think he'll be all right." She twisted her neck to look at him. "How are you?"

"I think I'll be all right. It's been a while since I've seen anything that bad." Which was very close to the truth—Bolan had seen isolated attacks on people by guerillas or bandits before, but it had been a long time since he'd seen such wholesale butchery as they'd witnessed in the village.

Kelleson's gaze turned distant for a moment. "Yeah, me, neither. You got any idea who might be behind this?"

"Not yet. How about you, Elliot?"

The security operative didn't turn, but stared out the window as he replied, his voice low, "I'm at a loss right now, but believe me, if I ever caught up with them, I might just give them the same treatment they gave those villagers."

For once, Bolan completely agreed with the other man. Even Kelleson nodded. "Okay, someone, for whatever reason, wanted to wipe that village off the map. Who the hell would do that and why?"

Bolan exchanged a covert glance with Morgan, pretty sure his seatmate had come up the same conclusions he had, but again he kept them to himself—there'd be time soon to have that discussion.

Morgan shrugged. "The question remains, who had the most to gain by doing this? The Colombian military? Unlikely—they have no reason to slaughter their own people, there's no gain for them I can see—"

"Unless they want us to stumble upon this and sound the alarm. But who would they blame it on?"

Kelleson turned to look at the two men. "Rebels in the jungle, because if everyone died, they could make up any story they wanted. Except—"

"We have two living witnesses to dispute their story." Bolan pulled out his sat phone and sent a quick message. "I can check with my paper and see if the local media's making any noises about the military saying rebels are slaughtering natives, as far-fetched as that seems. While we wait for confirmation or denial, let's keep our options open."

"How so?" Morgan asked.

"Let's posit that we're dealing with a third party—who might that be?"

No one had anything remotely resembling an answer. The rest of the trip passed in relative silence, broken only by the fitful cries of the sleeping boy.

When they got close to the village, the late afternoon was darkening into night. Etienne had recovered some of his normal mood, but was still a far cry from the cheery man he had been that morning. Scooping the boy into her arms, Kelleson turned to the three men.

"Let's keep our stories brief and matching. We came to the village to find it wiped out, with only these two surviving. We're trying to contact the authorities in the region to get someone here to investigate. Etienne, pull off the road here, and bring the others up so we can explain the story to them."

Etienne pulled over, and waited for the other SUV to pull up alongside. Kelleson explained the plan over the protests of the other students, but she was immovable. "This is the way it has to be. You can all help by keeping the villagers calm and focused on their day-to-day tasks. Above all, don't spread or confirm any rumors. If anyone asks you about what happened at the village, tell them the truth—other than what we've said about it, you don't know. Any questions?" she asked, looking hard at each of the students' faces. "Okay, let's get going."

With dismayed looks and much grumbling, the two SUVs accelerated toward the village. When they arrived, Kelleson got out, with Nampa still cradled in her arms.

"I'm gonna set him up in my hut for now, and see if I can get ahold of Medina. You guys go with Etienne and make sure the villagers are informed and calm. We'll catch up later, okay?"

Bolan frowned as she walked toward her hut. He'd hoped to pool his knowledge with Morgan as soon as possible, but that would have to wait. He fell into step beside Morgan, who stared at him with a speculative expression.

"You get any messages on your cell phone lately?" he asked Bolan.

"Yesterday I got a message from my family, asking how I was doing? Why?"

"Receive anything from work?" Morgan stared directly at him.

"Yeah, as a matter of fact I did. They let me know that you and I seem to be working on the same side, if for different masters."

Morgan nodded. "Yeah, that doesn't surprise me. You came up just like your jacket said you would, but in the village you were pure operative. Don't worry—your secret is safe with me. I'd say the next step is to pool our resources, except we should probably watch out for Nancy Drew there."

Bolan glanced over his shoulder at her hut. "Agreed. I think she could use a good night's sleep after this, so let's make sure she gets it. Etienne, too—I think the scene this afternoon kind of messed him up."

Morgan nodded. "And afterward, you and I can trade stories around the campfire."

# 15

Alec Hachtman sat very still in his tent, trying to calm the butterflies in his stomach as he made sure no beads of sweat were visible on his face.

He was in front of his laptop, connected by satellite video link with the board of directors of Paracor, who were pressing him on how the project was going and when they would be able to announce that the area was open to surveyors. Among the attendees was his superior, Mr. Ravidos, as well as a local representative for the company, Alfredo Roldos, a smooth-talking Ecuadorian in a suit that Hachtman bet cost more than he made in a month.

Hachtman was no stranger to high-pressure presentations. However, this one—which could make or break his career with the company—had been thrown together in the last ninety minutes to give to the entire board. It gave new meaning to the expression "thrown into the shark tank."

"In summary, gentleman, we are proceeding on schedule and expect to have the entire area cleared out according to the timetable that you can see on your monitors."

"This is very good news, indeed, Mr. Hachtman," Mr. Ravidos said. "Are there any follow-up questions, gentlemen?"

"I got one for your fair-haired wonder boy." The speaker was an older man with piercing, light blue eyes. He was one of the new guard on the board, named Mr. Seiver. Not much scared Hachtman, but this man did. "Something that's been bugging me ever since the board approved this harebrained scheme. We pay to clear the rights to this tract of land, send good men down there to clean the place out for the oil companies. But what if there isn't any oil in the ground? Did we just waste several million dollars for nothing?"

Hachtman restrained his smile—the old man had just played right into his hands. "An excellent question, sir. You've all seen the preliminary reports filed on the area that indicate trillions of barrels of oil down here. The international companies will be doing whatever they have to, to get at it, and we'll be here to make sure that their multibillion-dollar investments are safe and sound—"

Hachtman held up his hand to forestall Mr. Seiver's protest. "And in the unlikely event that the oil here is less than predicted, or it isn't cost-effective to recover, we have already identified logging and mining companies that will be falling over themselves to reap the unspoiled bounty down here. Mr. Ravidos will bring up the report on the alternate clients from around the world. As you can see, we already have timber companies submitting early bids to clear-cut the forest so the oil companies can set up their operations, thereby profiting twice off the same tracts of land. I can assure you, gentlemen, that our investment here will pay off handsomely, no matter whom we lease the mineral or logging rights to."

The reaction from the board in general seemed to be positive, with most of the members nodding and muttering to each other. Mr. Ravidos caught Hachtman's gaze, smiled and nodded.

"I don't know," another board member said. "Given the current administration, I can hardly see the governments of both the U.S. and Ecuador not looking into the wholesale pillaging of the rainforest."

Mr. Ravidos leaned forward. "Don't concern yourself with the U.S.—they've got enough problems on their plate to be worrying about this. As long as the oil keeps flowing, they'll guzzle it and keep demanding more. As for the Ecuadorian government, we've made sure that everything has been taken care of on that end, right, Mr. Roldos?"

"That is correct. The contracts have been signed and are on file at the Carondelet Palace as I speak. For all intents and purposes, Paracor Security has the legal right to exploit the land as we see fit, granted to us by the sovereign nation of Ecuador. Any claim to the contrary can be tied up in the courts down here for years, gentlemen."

Hachtman nodded, the man's line of reasoning paralleling his own. He didn't care what the company did with this tract of wilderness, as long as they made enough money off it to guarantee him a big promotion and private office back in the States.

"Mr. Ravidos, I have serious reservations about proceeding with this project." The new speaker was one of the younger board members with styled, black hair who always wore expensive suits. Hachtman had pegged him as a relative of one of the major shareholders, so he was surprised to see him taking this adversarial stand. "I've reviewed all of these reports, and I feel there is too much inherent risk involved in parceling these rights to third parties for exploitation. If it is found out that Paracor owns the holding company that controls the rights companies have leased and that we're supplying security for, at the least we'd be charged with conflict of interest and possible price-fixing."

Mr. Ravidos didn't even acknowledge his words with a glance. "You let me worry about those details. In the twenty-first century, gentlemen, good business is where you find it—and where you make it. We've invested a great deal of money, time and effort into creating this operation, and it has to produce tangible results, period. Unless someone has a *real* reason why we should suspend this operation, instead of a weak stomach—" he glared at the young board member, who looked away in embarrassment "—then it will continue as scheduled. Thank you for your time, Mr. Roldos, Mr. Hachtman."

"You're welcome, Chairman, and thank you." Hachtman

kept his eyes on Mr. Ravidos and wasn't surprised to see the
man move his hand back and forth on the polished tabletop,
the gesture clear. *Eliminate all potential witnesses.* His acknowledging nod was barely perceptible, but the other man
replied with a minute nod of his own. "Gentlemen, if you'll
excuse me, I have much to do here."

Breaking the connection, Hachtman brought up an audio
file on his computer that the mercs' comm man had sent him.
He listened to the female voice, a Nancy Kelleson of something called SARE, trying to raise Major Medina, saying that
there had been a terrible accident at one of the local villages.

Hachtman quickly dialed another number, voice-only this
time. "Good afternoon, Mr. Gamboa, how are you? This is
Mr. Hachtman....Yes, of Paracor Security....I'm well, thank
you....I'm afraid that I am calling with some unfortunate
news regarding the village on the edge of the border with Colombia....Yes, you've just heard? Well it seems that some of
the local volunteers from that relief group, the South American Relief Effort, were poking around the area...it seems
that they were there for a particular reason. I cannot be sure
if it was some kind of insurrection, but it wouldn't be the
first time foreigners had entered the country to stir up trouble....How? One of my security personnel had heard about
the incident and had traveled there to investigate, to make
sure we were not in danger....Yes, when he arrived, he saw
them in the area....I wouldn't care to speculate what they
might have been doing there, but I wanted to pass this on so
you could follow up if necessary...I'm afraid I don't know if
they are still in that other village nearby, but I assume that
the city of Nueva Loja will have that information....If you
wouldn't mind, I'd like to be informed so we can also be
on our guard....Yes, I will certainly let you know if we see
any unusual behavior....Thank you, Mr. Gamboa, I'll be in
touch."

Hanging up, he pressed a speed-dial number and the
person on the other end answered on the first ring. "Kapleron? I have another task for you and your men. I'm sending

you the coordinates of that village where the volunteers are
located....Yes, I've sent the army over to 'collect' them. It
seems the SARE people have been up to a lot more than just
helping the local villages....That's right, you're to go there
and make sure the volunteers never make it out alive. If the
army takes care of them, fine, otherwise, you handle it....
Good, contact me when you're finished."

Hachtman leaned back in his chair, comfortable with the
results of his misdirection, if not completely satisfied. While
he wasn't sure the army could react properly to the "revela-
tion" that the volunteers might be behind the massacre at
the village, the inference had been planted and it was up to
them to respond. The long history of *agents provocateurs* in
the region, combined with the disappearances his company
was behind, almost guaranteed that the volunteers would be
handled less than politely. Tempers would flare, and someone
was bound to provoke an incident. And if they didn't, Kapleron and his men would certainly be happy to finish the job.

A drop of cold, smelly water plopped from the ceiling onto
Hachtman's forehead. And the sooner they do, the sooner I
can get out of here and back to civilization, he thought.

**16**

Kelleson sat on her bed in her hut, trying to make sense out of everything that had happened. They had gotten back to the village by nightfall, and she had sworn the students to secrecy, not wanting news of the slaughter to get out and panic the rest of the village.

Unfortunately, that left her with the unenviable job of carrying the burden of what she'd seen by herself. She couldn't stop wondering what had happened in that village. Who would be behind such a travesty? And she had no idea what was up with Morgan and Cooper. One moment they were sniping at each other, the next working together as though they were soldiers in the same unit. There was some kind of unspoken understanding between them, and she was going to find out what it was.

Across from her, Nampa gobbled the last of his stew that one of the students had brought. Kelleson knew she should eat, but had only managed to choke down a few bites before giving the rest of hers to the hungry boy.

A knock on the door frame broke her reverie, and she glanced up to see Cooper in the doorway, holding a bottle of water. "Hey."

"Hi, come on in."

"Thanks." He offered her the bottle, nodding at the boy, who regarded them both with wide eyes. "I wasn't sure if you had anything left to drink in here—he seemed like he'd been stuck in that hut for days."

"Right, thanks." Kelleson opened the cap and took a quick swallow, not wanting to be impolite. She held it out to Nampa, who grabbed it and drained half of it in large swallows. "So, what now, Matt?"

"The best thing to do would be to get some rest, and we'll talk to the authorities tomorrow morning. Etienne's still having trouble raising them. I don't know if its due to sunspots interfering with the transmissions, or just the jungle itself, but we'll inform them as soon as we can, even if we have to go see them ourselves."

"All right…" A frown crossed Kelleson's face as a thought just struck her. "Matt, this is going to sound crazy, but…you don't think Morgan's somehow involved in what went on there, do you? I mean, there's something not right about him, but I can't put my finger on it."

The black-haired man shook his head. "No—his reaction to what he saw was as real as yours or mine was."

Kelleson could vouch for herself, but regarding the other two men, she wasn't so sure. Getting up, she walked over to him. "I appreciate you handling the situation so well back there. I know this is a dangerous place, but that sort of thing certainly isn't something you see every day." She placed her hand on his chest, feeling him breathe underneath her fingertips. "I just wanted to say I'm glad you're here."

The big American placed his hand over hers, and for a moment their eyes met and locked. Kelleson gazed up at him, lips slightly apart, just waiting. He bent tentatively, but just before his mouth touched hers, a shout from outside made his head snap up and look back at the door.

"Hey, Cooper, what's taking so long in there?"

A grimace flashed across his lean, handsome features. "That guy has the worst way of interrupting just about everything." Realizing she was still there and listening, he said. "Sorry, I didn't mean—"

"That's all right, go see what he wants. Perhaps later you

can stop by and we can talk." Kelleson smiled and increased her pressure on his chest, moving him toward the door. "Get going, otherwise he'll think we're up to no good in here."

"I'll be back to check on you both later." With that he turned and headed outside. Kelleson turned back to see Nampa polish off the bottle of water. His head lolled back and forth in the hammock, and she walked over to catch him just before he slumped over, unconscious. She checked his pulse, which was slow, but strong and steady.

Kelleson had been right—he'd drugged the water. She had detected a slight aftertaste in that first sip, even above the chlorine, and had kept her tongue over the opening when she had pretended to drink more.

She wasn't worried about Nampa. Even though the tranquilizer was probably a strong dose, he'd also just eaten a large meal, so it would affect him more slowly, as most of his blood would be aiding his digestion. Besides, after the horrors he'd seen, an uninterrupted night's sleep was probably the best thing for him right now, she thought. Plus, it got him out of the way so that she could pursue her own agenda.

Creeping over to the doorway, she leaned out just far enough to see Morgan and the supposed journalist sitting near the fire, their faces half-lit by the flickering orange-gold flames. Morgan held a stainless-steel flask out to the other man, who took it and had a quick drink, then handed it back. "That's not modified, too, is it?"

"Nope—would be a damn shame to adulterate good Scotch whisky like that." Morgan jerked a thumb over at the second tent in the clearing. "I took care of Etienne, he's sound asleep in there. How'd it go with Nancy?"

Cooper glanced over his shoulder, making her duck out of sight. "No problem. She'll be out in a minute or two, so keep your voice down for the time being." He took a deep breath, then let it out while staring into the flames. "Some mess we've gotten into here, isn't it?"

"Damn right. I was supposed to come over here to make sure the oil company my bosses work with is safe and sound, not get mixed up in some kind of crazy massacre. How 'bout you? I mean, what—you're with the Agency, right? You got the moves."

"You're good. Yeah, we'll call it the Agency. It's funny—your mission and mine aren't that far apart. I got assigned down here to make sure the locals weren't messing anything up—and now it seems that's exactly what they're doing." With a grin, he reached for the proffered flask again. "Isn't this area a bit far away from the oil fields?"

Morgan shrugged. "Supposedly you and I are sitting on one of the largest untapped oil reserves in the world. The company I'm working for was supposed to already have geologists and engineers surveying for test drilling sites, but the board of directors wanted to make sure the area was absolutely safe. Apparently one of them saw that *Tip of the Spear* documentary about those missionaries getting themselves killed in the sixties and thinks the same thing could happen again down here—only to oil workers whose families will sue the company. That's why I'm out here getting eaten alive with the likes of you instead of luxuriating in the two-star hotel back at Neuva Loja."

Cooper grinned again. "Well, before you head back to the lap of luxury, we should at least try to figure out what the hell is going on. I can't help feeling the hunters I ran into the first night I was here are connected to what happened at the village, but I'm not sure how."

"Oh, was that during your 'morning constitutional'?"

"Yeah, I didn't think I'd fooled you with that excuse. I was retrieving something that had been delivered for me, and ran into a hunting party—at night. The strange thing was, they were armed with dart rifles, as if they wanted to capture whatever animal they were hunting alive. I took one out and evac'd before the others discovered him."

Morgan held out both hands, as if weighing the evidence. "Okay, big-game hunters in the jungle in one hand and a slaughtered village in the other. I'm not really connecting the dots."

Cooper grimaced. "I said I didn't know how they were connected—I just think they somehow are. The problem is that they're out there somewhere, in several thousand square miles of jungle, and at the moment, I don't have a clue who they are or where they might be. I'd planned to gain the villagers' trust, then question them about what they might have seen recently. What we found this morning, however, accelerates my timetable to immediately. If someone's running around slaughtering villagers, then they gotta be stopped."

Morgan stared into the flickering fire. "Like you said, whoever's messing around here has to be stopped, but first you gotta know where to look."

"Yeah, I got some people working on that angle right now. Should have some idea where to begin pretty soon."

"Good, 'cause I want in if you go after them. Before we'd stumbled upon the massacre, I was going to ask Nancy if she'd heard anything about any missing people, since she'd been here longer than either of us. What do you think about our fearless leader?"

Kelleson leaned out a bit further, as curious about Cooper's answer as Morgan no doubt was.

"It seems our Nancy Kelleson has a rather checkered past. I thought the name sounded familiar, and when my superiors downloaded her file, I found out why. It seems she'd left England four years ago after a scandal involving an inappropriate relationship she'd had with a college student at Winchester when she was a teacher's aide. Although nothing was ever proven, she was fired and left the country nine months later. Apparently we now know where she ended up."

Kelleson leaned back into the hut, clenching her fists at the casual way the two men discussed the event that had destroyed her former life. Trying to shake off her anger and shame, she wiped tears from her eyes and focused on the conversation again.

Morgan's reply was cut off by shouts and screams coming from the far end of the village, making both men turn and look in that direction. A revving diesel engine could be heard, and then a short, popping burst from an automatic rifle cracked through the night.

"Galils." Drawing a pistol from behind his back, Morgan jumped to his feet, nodding toward Kelleson's hut. "Wake them?"

Cooper also drew a pistol from his back. "No point. We need to fall back and recon right now to find out who's messing with the village. Follow me."

The two men disappeared into the jungle, leaving a very perplexed Kelleson behind. She didn't know what to make of two undercover agents in her village. Had they brought whatever's going on in the area down on her people? Whatever the case, one thing was certain, she was also going to find out what was happening with her villagers. Sparing a quick glance at Nampa, still sleeping soundly in her bed, she snuck out of the hut. She silently promised she would not let him get taken by them—whoever they were.

Slipping into the dark forest, Kelleson weaved between the trees and plants, careful not to make a sound. Morgan and Cooper were both good, for although she proceeded cautiously, listening for noise every few yards, she didn't hear anyone ahead. But she had been here long enough to know how to move quietly. Besides, it would've been hard to make enough noise to be heard over the racket in the village.

The noises from the village—shouts and cries, mostly—suddenly quieted, and as Kelleson kept circling around the village's perimeter, she heard a familiar voice that made her heart sink. *Oh, no. Tell me he's not involved in this.*

"Villagers, it saddens me to inform you that the 'volunteers' you have been living with, who claimed to be here under the pretense of helping you, are working against our peaceful nation. They have come here using the cover of peaceful volunteers to attack you and your fellow citizens."

Kelleson crept forward until she could duck under a large fern, using it as cover to peek into the town square. What she saw made her gasp.

Everyone had been herded into the middle of the village,

men, women and children packed together in a tight cluster. In the center of the clearing was the APC, squat and menacing, its harsh spotlights casting a white glare over everything. Four of the volunteers knelt on the ground, hands clasped on their heads. Soldiers of the Colombian Army guarded both groups, Galil rifles leveled and ready. One of the boys—*Tom*, Nancy thought—must have tried to resist the soldiers, gaining a swollen, bruised cheekbone and a glazed look in his eyes. Calley Carter's shoulders trembled as tears streamed down her face, with Susanna Tatrow next to her, white-faced but defiantly staring at her captors.

Major Medina, dressed in his usual immaculate uniform, strode in front of them, then turned on the heel of his polished boot and walked toward the villagers, who were huddled together a few yards away.

The preening military officer stopped in front of them. "I cannot fault any of you for not knowing who and what you have harbored here. Indeed, I owe you an apology for coming into your village and frightening your women and children. However, I see that there are only five of the so-called volunteers here. Three are missing—and I want them. If you give them to me now, no harm will come to your village. But, if I find out you are hiding them from me, I will be very displeased."

Kelleson was just about to step out and announce herself when a hand clamped around her mouth. A strong arm encircled her waist, hauling her backward into the jungle. Writhing and squirming, she lashed out with her foot, connecting solidly with her attacker's shin and making him grunt in pain.

"Nancy. Nancy, it's us, Matt and Elliot! Stop fighting!" The whispered voice made her relax, and the arm around her loosened enough that she could turn to confirm who had snatched her. Sure enough, Morgan was there, rubbing his shin, and Cooper, too.

"Jesus Christ, are you trying to get us all killed?" she stormed.

Morgan glared right back at her. "No, we're trying to make sure you didn't run out there to get shot. I knew I heard someone else out here." He turned to Cooper, frowning in disgust. "Nice job with the tranquilizer, by the way."

Kelleson held up her hand. "Not this again—I was on to you, too, slick. Do either of you have a plan for freeing the kids and the village?"

The two men exchanged glances, then Cooper spoke. "Yes, but I need to get some gear from my tent first. With darkness on our side, we should be able to take them out fairly easily."

Kelleson shrugged Morgan's arm off. "All right, get whatever crap you need, and let me provide the distraction. And don't worry about me—I can take care of myself."

Before either of them could stop her, Kelleson stood and walked through the jungle, hands raised above her head. "Don't shoot! I'm coming out!"

Two of the nearest soldiers spun and aimed their rifles at her. Kelleson walked into the halogen lights, hands up, moving slowly and deliberately so as not to provoke a fatal reaction from any of the soldiers.

Medina whirled at the sound of her voice, and a predatory smile curved his mouth when he saw her. "Nancy, I'm so pleased we didn't have to come after you. Where are the other two men?"

Her hands still raised, Kelleson shrugged. "I'm not sure. When they heard you at the village, they took off into the jungle."

The major shook his head, much like a parent catching a child in a lie. "Please, lower your arms. You're sure you have no idea where they are?"

Kelleson waved at the verdant foliage surrounding them. "They're somewhere out there. Anything more, and your guess is as good as mine."

"I see." Medina swept the clearing with his piercing gaze. "Does anyone else know where the other two volunteers are? This is your last chance."

Kelleson kept her eye on the volunteers, all of whom were staring either at her or the army officer. Tatrow caught her eye and nodded slightly in the direction of the hunting camp, a quizzical look on her face. Kelleson shook her head ever so slightly in return. The last thing she wanted was for Medina to find the camp with the two survivors of the massacre, or Etienne, for that matter. If he was still out there, as well, they might have a chance.

Tatrow caught her nod, and her face darkened even further, but she said nothing. Beside her, Carter looked as if she might speak up, but Kelleson saw Tatrow nudge her and she clamped her mouth shut.

Medina sighed, then turned to address the jungle, raising his voice as he did so. "Americans! If you can hear me, I advise you to surrender peacefully, and I give you my word that no harm will come to you. If you do not surrender, I will be forced to take measures to draw you out, measures that will result in the injury or death of your compatriots. I do not want to do this, but I will if necessary. You have five minutes to come out of the jungle, otherwise I will be forced to injure one of your fellow volunteers." He stalked back to Kelleson. "If you have any influence over your friends, I suggest you exert it now."

She stared down at him. "Like I said, I don't know where they are."

His eyes narrowed as he glared at her, then he nodded to two of his men. "Escort Nancy to her hut and keep her there." His gaze traveled down her body. "We will have that conversation I mentioned earlier, and perhaps you will be more inclined to help me afterward."

The two men grabbed Kelleson's arms and pulled her toward her hut. As she was forced along, she glanced back at the jungle where she had last seen Morgan and Cooper, but caught no sign of them in the unbroken wall of trees.

**17**

M-4 in hand, Bolan had almost reached his launch point when he froze in his tracks, then hit the ground.

A few yards ahead, Bolan spotted a man dressed in tiger-stripe camouflage from head to foot sneaking around the corner of the tent. The man's back was to him, so Bolan couldn't see who it was. The other thing that caught his attention was the long barrel of the assault rifle the man held.

Bolan wondered where he'd come from. Was he part of the second unit of soldiers?

Their original plan had been simple—Morgan would circle to the southwest of the village while Bolan headed northwest to retrieve his gear. After five minutes, each one would be in position to move on the soldiers. Bolan would create a distraction with his better firepower, drawing off as many of the Colombian soldiers as possible while Morgan made for the 12.7 mm gun on the APC. However, that plan was presently in the crapper with the arrival of this new group of hostiles.

Slipping his night-vision goggles down over his eyes, Bolan turned them on and activated the thermal vision option. The world turned to bright colors, the nearby foliage a uniform orange and yellow, with the shape of the large tent next to him a darker red tone. On the other side, the form of the man he had just seen was clearly outlined against the wall of the tent in bright orange. Bolan hit the wireless connection on his smartphone and speed-dialed Morgan's number.

"Yeah?" the other man whispered.

"I'm at the tent, but we've got new players in town."

"I just spotted a tango on my side, up a tree," Morgan told him. "Tiger-stripe cammies and mask, long-barreled rifle, the works. Who the fuck are these guys?"

"I'm not sure, but I think they both might be connected to the hunters I ran into the day before yesterday. Can you take your man out?"

"What? Hey, it's one thing to back you up, it's another to directly engage a superior enemy. Remember, this village isn't my mission—finding out who's wiping out the other villages is."

"Yeah, well don't forget," Bolan reminded him, "Medina is fingering us for that very thing right now. We've got two choices, Elliot—either surrender and risk getting ourselves jailed or killed, neither one being the outcome *I* want, or try to save the volunteers and prevent an international incident."

"Wrong, there's also the third option—you and I hightailing it out of here to restart our investigation elsewhere. These people were in the wrong place at the wrong time, that's all. Odds are Medina will simply toss them in jail, and the U.S. or their own NGO'll bail them out in a month or two."

"That 'wrong place' you're referring to is the home of a lot of people who didn't ask for this shit storm to rain down on their heads. Look, I don't have time to debate—either you're in or out, right now."

"My guy's too far away—he's already in the trees. I don't have the range, and I'm damn sure not going to take him on from here."

"Okay, new plan. If they're covering the village from the north, they have a clear field of fire over everyone. See if you can circle around them and come up from behind. I just need you to provide a distraction, no need for any Rambo-style heroics. I'll try to get to the machine gun on the APC instead, then maybe we can dictate terms to these assholes. Wait for my mike, you won't miss it. Keep your head down and watch your six."

"I'll see what I can do. Morgan out."

Bolan checked the action on his M-4, making sure a round was ready to fire, then slung the carbine over his shoulder. Screwing the silencer onto the extended barrel of his pistol, he crawled to the rear of the tent. Unfolding his Leatherman, he slit the back seam of the tough canvas high enough to crawl through, finding himself amid the college boys' mess. The first thing he did was place the prepared Semtex explosive under one of the army cots, making sure he could activate the remote detonator with his phone.

Next he crept through the dirty clothes, coming across a small, almost empty bag of weed and smiling in spite of the circumstances, and kept moving toward the man on the other side of the tent wall. Just as he got there, there was a shout from the middle of the village.

"Two minutes left, Americans! Time is running out, both for you and your friends!" Major Medina shouted.

Bolan was about to reach out underneath the tent flap to grab the man's feet and send him crashing to the ground when the soldier turned and pushed open the tent flap to enter. Springing to his feet, Bolan leveled his pistol at the man's face.

"Don't move or you're dead."

The man's eyes widened in surprise, then he threw his assault rifle at Bolan, the stock slamming into his hand and knocking his aim off. Instinctively squeezing the trigger, Bolan's SIG Sauer spat out a round that punched a neat hole in the tent wall.

The masked man came in low as Bolan staggered backward, still trying to line up his sights on his opponent. Before he could draw a bead, the man was on him, grabbing the pistol and levering him backward until his legs hit one of the hammocks. Bolan went over on his back, hitting the earth with a breath-stealing thump, his pistol flying from his hands. His opponent jumped on top of him, hands searching for his throat as he settled on Bolan's chest to crush the air out of his lungs.

Already winded from his fall, Bolan struggled to suck in enough air to remain conscious. His vision blurred at the edges as the other man's grip tightened on his throat. One of his arms was pinned between the guy's leg and his torso, and he reached up to claw at the guy's face with his left hand, but his fingers slid off the hard face mask.

Just as Bolan's sight began contracting to a fuzzy gray tunnel, his hand scrabbled over the other man's mask and found his unprotected throat. Curling his fingers into the "ram's head" position Bolan threw a short punch directly at his enemy's Adam's apple. Taken by surprise, he choked as his throat seized up. The man's hold slackened for a moment, and that was all Bolan needed.

Twisting his upper body, he wrenched the merc's hands off his throat and shoved him off. The man tried to keep his grip, but Bolan squirmed out from under him, lashing out with his boot to slam him in the back of the head. The man pitched forward, but pushed up to his hands and knees, shaking his head and gagging. Coughing, himself, Bolan rose first to tackle his enemy, slamming his interlaced fingers into the back of the man's neck. He collapsed to the ground, with Bolan on top of him, and lay there, unmoving, one last breath wheezing out of him.

Checking for a pulse, Bolan found nothing. He quickly stripped the dead man of his fatigues and pulled them on, along with the guy's web belt, which contained two smoke grenades and three full magazines. Casting about for his SIG, he found it under a hammock, then located the man's rifle, another short-barreled Colt Commando 5.56 mm carbine, which he checked then held on to, stripping the body of three full magazines, as well. He opted to stick with his own NVG gear instead of the other man's headgear. In the heat of what he expected to be a distracting battle, he doubted anyone would notice the difference.

Bolan crept to the tent flap and listened for a moment

before heading out. Major Medina announced the one-minute warning, and Bolan used his shouting as cover to slip out of the tent and around the back, melting into the jungle to approach the APC from the soldiers' blind side.

Well, not totally blind, Bolan thought as he snuck through the thick foliage, stepping carefully to prevent vines from entangling his feet. The major was smarter than he'd figured, as there was not one, but two soldiers guarding the back side of the Urutu. One beret-wearing soldier was at the front corner of the vehicle, his Galil held at port arms as he divided his attention between his superior officer and the surrounding jungle. The other man posed the larger problem; he was standing with his head and upper body sticking out of a hatch on the APC's roof, rifle at the ready, snugged into the crook of his shoulder. Bolan didn't envy his exposed position one bit, especially with snipers in the area. He was only surprised that the man was still alive. He wondered what the other crew was waiting for.

The undercarriage of the APC was high enough off the ground that Bolan saw two of the huddled volunteers near the vehicle's solid bulk. That gave him an idea, and no sooner had he thought of it than he quietly slung his rifle and drew his silenced pistol. The distance from him to the soldier on the ground was about fifteen yards, an average-range shot for his pistol and surroundings. Under the cover of a large, broad-leaved fern, Bolan settled in on one knee, his SIG held steady in a two-handed Weaver grip, settling the three-dot sights on his target's chest. All he needed was the right opportunity.

Sure enough, like clockwork, he heard a shout from Medina. "Thirty seconds—"

The moment the army officer spoke, Bolan exhaled and squeezed the double-action trigger twice. His pistol coughed out two 180-grain subsonic bullets that smashed into the soldier's chest, crushing his breastbone and mushrooming through his heart and lungs, patching his fatigues with crimson as the man pitched forward, dead before he hit the ground.

As if that was the signal everyone had been waiting for, all hell broke loose around the village. Bolan had just started to move his pistol up to aim at the merc on the top of the APC when the crack of a high-powered rifle echoed across the clearing, and the man's body slumped over, blood and bone fragments spraying into the air from the bullet impacting his skull. The high pops of several Galils drowned out the booming single shots of the sniper rifles. Bolan also caught the sustained chatter of other assault rifles, probably the Colts from the second team, interspersed with the other weapons. Under it all he heard shouts and screams coming from the village square and saw running shapes flit in front of the Urutu. The important thing was that none of the firing seemed to be coming from this side of the APC.

Bolan broke cover and ran toward the huge, run-flat tire. Snaking out a hand, he grabbed the barrel of the nearby Galil rifle on the ground and dragged it to him without anyone taking a shot at him. Scrambling around to the other side, he lifted his night-vision goggles as he spotted three of the students, Carter, Saderson and Tatrow, all huddled under the APC.

"Hey, guys, back here!" Bolan shouted over the chattering of the nearby rifles.

"Cooper! What the hell are you—!"

"No time to explain, just get over here, damn it! Hurry up, before they get this thing moving." Bolan kept an eye on the exposed PTO rods, hoping they wouldn't get the vehicle started for another minute or so.

Tatrow didn't waste any time, but scrambled underneath the V-shaped hull, taking up a position at Bolan's shoulder. "Do you know how to shoot this?" He held up the rifle to the young woman.

She shook her head. "I've never even held one before."

"Okay—how about you, Saderson—Mike?" Bolan asked the college student who had urged Carter to scoot over ahead of him. Before the kid could answer, Bolan shoved him into the dirt. "Get down!"

One of the soldiers who had taken up a firing position near the passenger tire had noticed the three students escaping and was turning his rifle around to cover them. Bolan raised his pistol and shot first, the pair of bullets catching the soldier in the shoulder and side and sending him sprawling in the dirt.

Saderson picked himself up and looked back at the dead soldier. "Thanks, man."

Bolan was about to ask him the rifle question again when they heard a thump from the APC overhead, followed by a long rattling roar. Even from the opposite side, the gunfire was so loud it sounded as if it was shooting right through Bolan's skull.

"Someone got to the machine gun. We'd better get the hell out of here!" Bolan switched the Galil's fire selector to single-shot and held the rifle out to Saderson.

He took it and pulled back on the cocking lever, ejecting a fresh round. "Shot one of these in Las Vegas last year—I should remember how."

"Hey, what about that extra Colt carbine over your shoulder?" Carter asked, a determined frown on her face.

"Can you handle it, Calley?"

"Handle it? My grandfather, father and four brothers all hunt back in Michigan, plus I went to All-State in competitive shooting—you bet your ass I can handle it."

"These aren't deer, you know—they'll be shooting back." Bolan unslung the carbine and held it out.

"No shit! But I'm damn sure not gonna go out like a frightened tourist." The slim blonde checked its load with practiced ease. Bolan then gave her two additional magazines

"Okay, I'm first, Mike and Susanna next, Calley, you bring up the rear. One more thing…" Bolan pulled out his phone and peeled off a small, adhesive square of plastic, affixing it to the underside of the APC. "Follow me and keep your head down. Calley, keep an eye out behind us, and if you see anyone you don't recognize, stay low and shoot three rounds at them to keep their heads down, then take cover behind the nearest tree. I'll back you up in a second." Bolan pulled his goggles down, scanning the nearby forest with thermal vision. No obvious hostiles in the immediate area. He shoved the goggles back up just as the Urutu's diesel engines rumbled into life. "Everyone ready? Go, go, go!"

Leading the way, Bolan ran crouched over into the jungle, then turned as soon as he had reached the tree line to cover the others. No sooner had they left the protection of the armored personnel carrier than it lurched into motion, rumbling toward a hut in its path, the yammering machine gun spitting lead and fire on the other side. Bolan didn't stick around, but led the others deeper into the jungle, until they were at least fifty yards out. Taking cover behind the huge, exposed root structure of a massive tree, Bolan stood guard while the others caught their breath.

"Where're Nancy and the others?"

Tatrow shook her head. "Medina was walking toward her hut when the shooting started—I don't know what happened to Tom. The villagers all scattered at the first gunshot—almost like they knew the drill already."

Bolan grunted. "Probably closer to the truth than you think. Living in the middle of a place like this—where your neighbors are just as likely to shoot you as say hello—tends to hone your survival reflexes."

Saderson stared up at him, the assault rifle clutched in his hands. "Speaking of survival, namely ours, just what in the hell is going on here? That other village slaughtered, and now Colombian Army soldiers are coming after us—or should I say you?"

Carter frowned at him. "Hey, Mike, we were all at the village, so I don't see how he or anyone else is more culpable."

Tatrow snorted and looked at Bolan. "Yeah, but they wanted you and Elliot, that's why they used us as bait."

Bolan held up his hand. "Let's all calm down for a moment and think this through. Standard hostage-taking procedure is to get everyone in a particular group together for bargaining purposes, that's all. They didn't want us divided because then they wouldn't have control over everyone."

"Yeah, but when common sense would have said for you to surrender, instead you come out of the jungle, guns blazing. What the hell was up with that?"

"Let's just say I didn't have any intention of being taken hostage." Bolan holstered his pistol and unslung his Colt, checking its load. "And I sure as hell wasn't going to let you guys go through that, either, if I could help it. Now everyone just be quiet for a minute." He listened for any sounds of combat in the distance. The gunfire had died down, but he heard the growl of the APC engine as it faded away.

"All right, assuming Medina and Nancy are still alive, they're probably in the APC getting the hell out of the fire zone," Saderson said.

"And where'd you get that weird mask?" Carter asked.

"The same place I got the fatigues and the assault rifle—off a dead guy. Now stop asking questions and let's get you guys to safety. The best place to go will be a few klicks away from the village. I'll get you to a place to set up camp for the night and then we'll figure out the next step—probably getting you guys out of here and back to Nueva Loja. It's too risky to have you stay here with everything that's going on around here."

Tatrow frowned. "As if we even had any clue what that was."

Bolan stared at her, a small smile creasing his lips when she drew back at his alien appearance. Although the night-vision goggles weren't designed with intimidation in mind, the strange facade had that effect on most people.

Carter piped up. "What about Nancy? And Elliot?"

"Elliot can take care of himself, Calley. And I've got a way to track where Nancy's going, as well, so we'll get her back. Let's get moving. I'm taking point, so I'll be a few yards ahead. Stay alert, but watch me, as well. If I do this—" Bolan raised his clenched right fist in the air "—take cover as quickly and quietly as you can." He rousted the tired college kids and began plotting a path into the jungle with his cell phone, making sure to stay well away from the village site.

At least he hoped Elliot could handle himself back there....

## 18

As Morgan surveyed the chaos in front of him, he couldn't believe how bad things had gone.

Their revised plan had been a decent one, with Morgan firmly committed to keeping his head down and providing a distraction, letting Cooper risk his neck to get to the machine gun on the APC. If he could have somehow managed that, they might have been able to force Medina and his unit to surrender.

Morgan had spent most of the allowed time working his way around the village. He had almost been in position when he had spotted the camouflaged soldier adjusting his position among the low-hanging branches of the tree he had been planning to use as cover for his first volley.

Freezing in place, he'd scooted back into the brush as his sat phone had vibrated softly in his cargo pocket. Hitting his wireless earpiece, he'd informed Cooper of the new company. They'd come up with the contingency to dispatch him, and Morgan was in business again. Cooper's words had rankled him, however—he was well aware of the costs the villagers might have to pay. Life was tough all over. He couldn't get involved—he had his own mission to finish.

As he sat in the jungle, waiting, the memory of those kids snatching the melting chocolate from Cooper's hand rose in his mind. That was followed by images of the massacre at the other village, including the murdered children there. Elliot sighed in frustration, knowing what he had to do. Shit, I must be getting soft in my old age, he thought. All right, Cooper, you'll get your distraction—but where's your damn signal?

As if on cue, the whole scenario suddenly turned to shit. As he was about to work his way into a better position, the sniper above him suddenly fired, the shot echoing out over the jungle. The shooter followed up with another bullet into the mass panic that had rippled out among the people in the clearing.

Morgan had to hand it to Medina—he may have been an arrogant ass, but the man knew how to maintain military discipline. Barking orders to his men, he quickly established fire points and mustered a withering return of bullets that shredded the tree above Morgan, raining bits of leaves and broken branches down on his head. He hunched into the plants surrounding him, sure there would be a much larger weight crashing to the ground nearby. But when no body fell, he poked his head up just in time to hear another rifle shot crack out above him.

Realizing he couldn't get anything done while the sniper was around, Morgan looked up, hoping to spot the man, but couldn't see him through the thick leaves. The tree the shooter had picked for his station was covered in a thick latticework of vines, so Morgan holstered his pistol, grabbed a handful and hung off the thick green ropes to test them. When they didn't break, he started climbing. Soon he was ten yards off the ground and slowed his ascent to better take the sniper by surprise.

Scattered bursts of gunfire still came from the clearing, and Morgan was careful to stay behind the thickest part of the trunk. Even with the steel-cored 5.56 mm rounds coming his way, the tree's diameter had to be a yard, maybe a yard and a half. Still, when a stray bullet whizzed by, neatly severing a nearby branch as large as his thumb, Morgan wondered what the hell he was doing up there in the first place.

One last heave and he entered the thicker foliage, surrounded by a supposedly protective canopy of green. The only problem then was that he had to work his way around to see—and shoot—the sniper without getting capped first.

Slowly, Morgan crawled through the branches, trying to move whenever a shot rang out, then waiting until the sniper fired again. He craned his neck as far around the tree as he could, wishing he had a shotgun so he could just point and shoot.

He levered himself over another thick branch and froze, one arm outstretched to grab the next limb. The sniper was four yards below him, stretched out on two branches that grew parallel to each other out from the trunk—a natural shooting platform. Intent on his prey, he squeezed off another shot without noticing Morgan above him. The man steadied his sleek, matte-black sniper rifle, then returned to searching for his next victim through the mounted scope.

The real problem was that Morgan was in a terrible position to take the shot—off balance and at a bad angle. But he didn't dare try to improve it. If the sniper noticed any movement from above, it would all be over very quickly. Morgan slowly moved his free hand toward his pistol, inch by inch, until he grasped the butt. Making sure he had a tight grip, he drew it and extended his arm, taking a bead on the upper portion of the man's back. He tried to steady his breathing, but his muscles already ached from holding the awkward position this long, making his gun hand tremble.

The sniper fired again, and as the echo of the shot boomed around them, Morgan squeezed his pistol's trigger three times. The 9 mm hollow-point slugs burrowed into the sniper's neck and shoulders, and he slumped forward. Morgan descended through the canopy until he reached the body, then put another slug into the back of his head. Keeping his pistol trained on the gunman, he cleared his hands from the weapon, then checked the guy's pulse until he was sure the other man was dead.

Another booming shot made Morgan's head snap up. Another shooter! Holstering his pistol, he grabbed the rifle—a customized Galil 7.62 mm with a high-powered scope, skeletonized stock and extended barrel—and hunkered down over the other sniper's body, scanning in the direction of the shot through the scope. Another shot exploded through the clearing, drawing a furious hail of return fire. Morgan swept the trees, hoping to see another camouflaged form tumble out of one of them, but his search was not rewarded with a crumpled body on the ground. So instead he looked for a tree whose leaves looked as though they were just shot to hell....

About sixty yards away was a tree practically identical to the one Morgan was in, right down to the tattered leaves and broken branches on the side facing the village. He snugged the weapon into his shoulder, about to shoot blind, when an earsplitting roar erupted from the APC on the other side of the clearing. The other tree shook under the high-powered bullets, branches and leaves disintegrating under the assault. Morgan peered through the scope, unable to look away as the front of the tree was raked back and forth, up and down by the machine gunner. Within the cloud of pulverized wood and leaves, he saw a dark form fall off a branch and tumble end over end to the ground. The sight of the obviously dead sniper galvanized another thought in Morgan's mind. My position's next!

Dropping the rifle, he lunged for cover, praying he could get behind the trunk before the gunner opened up again. The branches and vines, which had been so easy to traverse on his way up, now were slippery under his groping touch. Pushing with his feet, he slithered along a branch and swung himself around the bulk of the tree just as the shooter began firing. Morgan didn't stop, but free-fell down the back side of the trunk, trying to slow his descent by snagging the vines without breaking a finger or hand. He slid a good ten yards before catching hold of a vine tight enough to stop him, just as high-caliber bullets punched through the tree trunk several yards above his head.

Glancing at the jungle floor a couple of feet below, Morgan let go and dropped to the ground, tucking and rolling away from the tree, then lying prone. He drew his pistol

the instant he stopped moving and twisted around to make
sure no one was coming after him from the clearing. The
sniper rifle lay on the ground nearby, and Morgan crawled to
it and slung the weapon over his shoulder. He gave a slow ten
count, then began moving east, parallel to the main square,
toward Kelleson's hut. With everyone else either dead or scattered into the jungle, she was the only hostage of value at this
point.

Slowing as he approached the latrine, Morgan gave the pit
toilet a wide berth as he passed. He saw the roof of Kelleson's
hut several yards beyond and headed for it. The gunfire from
the clearing had slackened considerably, but he heard some
kind of commotion from inside the building. Coming up on
the rear of the building, he stopped at the corner and risked a
quick glance in the rear window.

Inside, Kelleson struggled against two soldiers, while
Major Medina stood in the doorway. Although she probably
could have held her own against one of them, the pair had
her, one by each arm, and propelled her to the door.

"I'm very tired of your so-called volunteers coming in
and instigating rebellion at every chance they get. Since they
have chosen not to surrender, and have attacked me and my
soldiers, I am forced to interrogate you instead—and I guarantee you, it will not be fast and painless."

"You can't just leave these villagers to fend for themselves! You saw what happened out there, someone is trying
to kill everyone here! And you're just going to leave, you
coward!" Kelleson spit in Medina's face, earning a slap from
the smaller South American.

"Take her to the Urutu. There is no doubt that your so-
called friends are rebels who planned to attack us here
anyway. When we leave, they will have no reason to attack
the village. It is obvious your friends have come here to sow
anarchy among my people. It would be better for you now if
you would simply admit any connection with them—perhaps
I can convince the local judge to show leniency in exchange
for your cooperation."

"Go fuck yourself."

He shook his head. "Perhaps a few months in prison will make you more cooperative. Get her out of here."

Morgan weighed his options. There was no way he could save Kelleson the way things currently stood. Charging into an already pissed off army unit that had already been beaten once would only guarantee him a swift death. No, he had to retreat and regroup, then Cooper and he could figure out their next step.

Stepping carefully to the corner of the hut nearest to the clearing, he peeked out just in time to see Kelleson being wrestled into the APC. Bodies littered the clearing—soldiers, villagers and one T-shirt- and khaki-clad form that Elliot recognized as one of the volunteers. The others were nowhere in sight, giving him hope that they'd escaped. The reduced force of Colombian solders—only six by then—boarded the APC and roared out of the clearing, the wide tires rolling over several bodies as they left.

Morgan straightened and stretched his back, feeling the stress and pain of the last few minutes wash over him. He was about to step into the clearing when he felt a warm circle of metal press into the back of his neck and immediately knew what it was.

"Raise your pistol over your head, barrel pointing up," a voice said behind him. Morgan did as he was told, and his gun was pulled from his hand. The circle of metal stopped pressing into him. "Step backward, along the wall, keeping your hands away from your body. Do not try to run into the clearing or around the corner—that'll only get you shot. Come along now."

Morgan did so, knowing he couldn't possibly get to cover or out of range of the mystery gunman. "Who are you?"

"Just keep moving." The man had a slight European accent, but Morgan couldn't place his nationality. He kept listening, however, as the man radioed to someone else. "This is three—I have one of them. Affirmative, will rendezvous at site two. Cleanup is commencing? Good, make sure you collect everyone if possible. Three out."

Morgan kept backing up until he felt the gun muzzle again. "Now what?"

"We're going to take a walk. Place your hands behind your back. Do not try anything."

Morgan instinctively tensed as the man came up behind him, ready to try and swing at him once he had grabbed his hand to secure it. But as soon as the guy touched him, he kicked Morgan's legs out, sending him crashing to the ground. Before he could recover, the man knelt on top of him and lashed his wrists together with a plastic zip-tie. He then grabbed him by the arm and hoisted him back to his feet.

"Had to make sure you wouldn't try anything." The man brushed dirt and leaf mold off Morgan's face. "Now, let's take that walk, shall we?"

Prodded with the other man's pistol, Morgan was marched deeper into the jungle, with only one thought going through his head as he stumbled along—I sure hope Cooper made out better than I did.

# 19

Lying on the bare metal floor of the APC as it bounced through the jungle, Kelleson's head rang from the blows she had taken. Not only had Medina slapped her hard enough to draw blood, but she'd also banged her head twice coming in. The first time on the frame of the pressurized hatch she had been shoved through, the second when one of the soldiers had pushed her to the floor, making her head bounce off the steel and sending stars shooting across her vision.

The interior of the personnel carrier was dark and humid, smelling of stale sweat, unwashed bodies and the distinct odor of feces. Kelleson breathed through her mouth to avoid the horrible odor. She had landed next to what she thought was a wounded soldier, but as she looked closer she saw he was dead, a quarter of his skull blown away. Kelleson scooted into a corner of the APC, covering her mouth with her hand and trying to not throw up.

The major had entered the passenger space last and had knelt beside her, his mouth close to her ear. "When I'm through with you, you'll wish you had taken me up on my previous offer."

Kelleson gritted her teeth to still the ringing in her head as she stared back at him. "Not fucking likely, you bastard."

He didn't bother hitting her again, but stood and headed for the driver's compartment. "Watch her," he ordered two of the soldiers sitting in fold-down seats before disappearing into the front section, pausing only to wave at the corpse. "And cover him up, for God's sake."

Kelleson pushed against the wall to lever herself into a sitting position, trying to ignore her aching head. The two soldiers assigned to keep an eye on her were doing their duty perhaps a bit too well, their gazes roving up and down her body. Hugging her knees to her chest, she glared at them, not saying a word. The two men didn't say anything, either, but simply exchanged knowing glances.

The APC slowed and Kelleson and the soldiers in back all glanced up at the front of the vehicle, where a pitched argument was breaking out.

"I said just drive over it, Corporal!"

"I would, sir, but there is a strong chance that it will foul the PTO driveshaft, and then we'll be stuck out here until relief arrives. It would be safer to have the men clear the road."

"Damn it! What good is a mine-proof vehicle if it can't handle this godforsaken jungle?" Medina's head popped into the rear area. "A tree has fallen and is blocking the road. Private Romero, Private Vega, get out there and clear the road. Use the winch if you have to."

The two men saluted and scrambled to the side door. Medina nodded to another private. "Man the top hatch, make sure no one is trying to ambush us."

"Mind the blood," Kelleson called as the soldier opened the topside door and poked his head out, rifle at the ready.

A shout came from outside, and the man on the top called down. "Major, Private Romero says there are blast marks on the tree. He thinks it—"

"Private, what the hell is wrong with you?" Medina stormed into the passenger compartment just as the topside soldier's body fell to the floor, blood spreading over his fatigues and dripping onto the floor. His head lolled to one side, bright crimson leaking from his limp form.

Medina scrabbled for his holstered pistol as a small, olive-green canister fell into the room, spewing noxious smoke that made Kelleson's eyes water and her throat burn.

"Tear gas! We have to get out!" She scrambled past the other two soldiers to the back door, pushing on the release, but the panel refused to budge. "Medina!" She shouted between coughs. "Help me!"

Tears streaming from his closed eyes, the major pushed her aside and threw his weight against the door, shoving it open. He stumbled out to the road, then turned back and grabbed Kelleson, who was hacking so hard she could barely breathe. She fell to the ground, spitting in a vain effort to clear her throat, which felt like a tube of pure fire. She wanted to rub her eyes, but knew that would only make it worse. She felt other people push past her as the last two soldiers spilled out of the APC, one stepping on her hand during his clumsy effort to get free. Pistol shots exploded all around her, making Kelleson flinch and shy away from the loud noises. But there was nowhere to go.

Something hard was pressed into her hand, and she heard the slosh of liquid as her fingers closed around it. "Pour this over your face and eyes," a voice said. Almost crazy with pain, Kelleson did as ordered, feeling lukewarm water sluice over her itching, burning eyes, nose and mouth. The torturous effects of the gas faded, although her face still tingled and burned.

Kneeling on the ground, Kelleson sat back on her heels and rubbed more water into her face, washing as much of the chemical off as possible. The canteen was empty when she tossed it aside. Forcing her teary eyes open, she saw a short, bandy-legged man with a leathery face and crow's-feet at the corners of his watery blue eyes. He was dressed in tiger-stripe camouflage fatigues with a battered bush hat on his head. A knife hung on his olive web gear, handle down, and he held a smoking pistol in his other hand.

Kelleson looked around to see the remaining members of Medina's platoon sprawled on the ground, all shot through the head. Next to her was the major's body, his sightless eyes swollen shut, never to open again. She looked up to see other, similarly clad men standing in a loose semicircle around her, along with a familiar face—Morgan. His hands were behind his back, and he looked crestfallen.

"Who are you people, and what do you want?"

The short man addressed the others, never taking his eyes off her. "Clear the vehicle, wash it down and open the windows. We're riding back in style this time." He tossed her a gas mask. "You'll want to wear this on the trip back. Try to escape, and I'll shoot you in both kneecaps and tie you to the roof."

"I want to know who you are—or who you're working for—and where you're planning to take us."

The small man moved with deceptive speed, stepping forward and slamming the butt of his pistol into Kelleson's mouth. The shock to her already lacerated and burning lips made her fall back and moan, holding her fingers to her mouth in a futile attempt to soothe it.

*"Hou jou bek,"* he grunted. "Shut your mouth. You're the British bitch who poked her nose where it didn't belong, aren't you? Well, now you'll get the chance to see as much as you want." He nodded toward the Urutu. "Get 'em both inside and let's get moving."

Dazed, Kelleson didn't resist when she was hauled to her feet and pushed into the APC's hold again. Morgan followed right behind her. The stench of blood and lingering odor of tear gas almost made her vomit, and Kelleson fought to keep her rising gorge back. The gas mask forgotten, she collapsed into a folding seat and turned toward the wall, numbed to the terrible possibilities of what might lay in store for Morgan and herself.

**20**

Hachtman met the returning security squad as they drove in, his eyes widening at the obviously military vehicle they'd brought with them. While anxious to know how their mission went, he was careful not to show it to Kapleron.

The rumble of a large diesel engine was the first indication that the plan might not have survived first contact with the enemy intact. When the hulking, camouflaged, six-wheeled vehicle burst from the jungle foliage and skidded to a stop in the clearing, Hachtman was only moments away from hitting the evac code on his cell phone that would send everyone else into the bush. Only after Kapleron's head poked up out of the top hatch, boonie hat firmly jammed on his head, did Hachtman relax.

"Well, what d'ya think?"

"What do I—what the hell is this?" Hachtman's initial fear had been burned away by his growing anger. "Where did this come from?" He stalked closer, noticing the complex spray-painted insignia on the side: a plumed knight's helmet over a shield, its quadrants divided into red, yellow, purple and blue, with four red plumes surrounding it, two on either side. The motto underneath read *Paso de Vencedores*.

The businessman stared at the huge vehicle with a sinking feeling in his stomach. "Don't tell me you stole a Colombian Army military vehicle?"

Kapleron had been busy with something on the top of the

APC and only then looked at Hachtman. "Look out below!" he cried as he shoved a large human form, dressed in camouflage fatigues stained black, off the top. Hachtman jumped back as the dead body flopped to the ground, feeling the control he'd previously had over this operation slipping away.

"What is the meaning of this?"

"I didn't like the Range Rovers, so I traded up." Contrary to Hachtman's confusion, the little South African seemed overjoyed, almost ebullient as he cut the bodies of dead soldiers off the top of the vehicle and kicked them to the ground. "Relax, *baas,* we had to commandeer this vehicle when the Colombian Army took over the village. Besides, they'd already picked up someone you'll be very interested in."

When he'd removed the last of the vehicle's grisly cargo, Kapleron jumped to the ground and hammered on the side door with the butt of his knife. The steel panel opened, and a woman and man stumbled out. Off balance, the man fell to the ground, his hands secured behind his back. The woman moved to help him up, but was stopped by the other mercenaries spilling out of the APC.

"Damn it, leave me alone, you bastards!"

Hachtman's heart leaped when he recognized the woman's voice—she had been with the party investigating the village.

"Kapleron, get over here right now!" Hachtman's voice was on the ragged edge of hysteria. He was aware of the other mercenaries watching him with expressions ranging from disinterest to disgust, but didn't care.

Their leader took his time, inspecting parts of the APC before leaving it to walk slowly over to the scientist. "What do you want, *baas?*"

"I want your men to get these prisoners inside one of the tents and keep them under guard. Dispose of these bodies— preferably somewhere where they're never found—and get this vehicle under cover immediately. From you I want a complete report of what happened at the village—*right now.*"

"*Aweh,* man, just relax and let us finish our job out here."

"Finish—finish your job? From what I can see, you

haven't finished the first task I set to you. Where are the rest of the volunteers—everyone who was at the target village? The only thing I see you do is run around and kill anyone in your way! You couldn't even go to a defenseless village and pick up a half dozen fucking college kids!" Saliva flecked the other man's face, but Hachtman didn't care.

Kapleron removed a handkerchief from his shirt pocket and mopped his face off. Any traces of his former joy were gone, erased as if he had also wiped them off his features with the cloth. "You best be careful in this heat, *baas*. It can make you say crazy things."

The smaller man rocked back and forth on his heels. "I think it time you and I had a conversation to remind each other how things work here. My job—my *only* job—is t'make sure you are safe here and to carry out the company's directives in the best way that *I* deem appropriate, nothing more. Any other extracurricular activities were t'be done only if I deemed it safe and appropriate. So all the huntin' we did, all the sneakin' around the villages, all that was done only 'cause I wanted to. And the killin'—that happened 'cause I wanted it t'happen, as well. If you'd like to see if you ken stroll through the jungle to the evac point on yer own, then hop to it. All you have t'do is say the word, and me and my mates are gone, no worries. We'll see you on the dock—assuming you actually make it out alive."

The smaller man leaned forward, one stubby finger extended to poke Hachtman in the chest with each word, as if punctuating them. "As fer the dustup in tha' village, don't you *ever* try to tell me how t'do my job again! You have no idea what you're talkin' about, takin' on a platoon of Colombian soldiers, who, while sloppy and undisciplined, still managed t'kill three of my squad and almost got away with two of the folks you're all fired up to find! Just feckin' remember this—only me and my men stand between you and these trigger-happy Americans, and me and my men are the only people keeping you alive out here. Best you keep that in your head, otherwise, I ken stop doin' my job just as easily, *ja?*"

The mercenary's words had been delivered no louder than a regular conversation, but the sheer rage in them, particularly in the last sentence, took Hachtman aback. Too late, he realized just how right Kapleron was—if the security detail pulled out, he *might* be able to make it through the jungle to the pickup point, but GPS navigation was no match for a roadblock staffed with drug-addled rebels or hostile natives. All it would take is one bad encounter in the fifty-plus miles to the evac point to have his people taken hostage or killed. The squinty-eyed little bastard had Hachtman over a barrel, and the security man knew it.

Rubbing his breastbone where the merc had poked him, the tall businessman straightened and took a deep breath before replying. "I apologize if I cast any aspersions on your competence, or on that of your men. It wasn't my intent."

Kapleron eyed him for a moment, then nodded. "All right, then."

"The second man—what happened to him?"

"That other guy, he's pretty good—he got away from us. One of the volunteers was killed in the firefight, the rest either ran into the jungle, or were hidin' in the village somewhere. When we saw the girl get taken by the Colombians, we knew we had to get her back. I already had the man we brought in, see, so two out of the three ain't too bad. Besides, I got a feelin' we'll be seeing that second *bru* again, and soon."

"Why do you say that?"

"Me and him got some unfinished business. I think he was the one that killed Hans during our night hunt, and then the goddamn *doos* up and kills MacKenzie during the village op. Now, he might have gotten lucky once, but twice? No, he's not just some volunteer come to the jungle for kicks, he's some kind of agent or military, maybe an American, but he's obviously after something out here, and we need to make sure he doesn't find it."

"And how are you expecting to do that? I'm sure you most

likely left a trail even a blind ape could follow. If he is so dangerous, what are you going to do once he gets here?"

Kapleron's eyes narrowed as he regarded Hachtman, who actually leaned back upon seeing the look in the South African's eyes. "Now, when we have the advantage of surprise, I'm going to let him come in and see all he wants before I put a bullet right between his eyes."

## 21

Bolan led the students through the jungle—not deeper in, but back to the village instead.

Their destination had been the subject of a fierce but brief argument once the shooting had died down. He'd pushed for making a separate camp, then going back to find villagers for reinforcements, but had been overruled by the students, who'd said that people could be dying in the village right as they speak. In the end, the three volunteers had started heading off in the direction they thought the village was, leaving Bolan behind until he'd thrown his hands into the air and gone after them. After pointing them in the right direction, he led them back.

As they approached, he heard noises ahead—excited voices talking over one another, crying children and crooning women trying to calm them down.

Finding a large tree they could all hide behind, Bolan held up his right fist, gratified to see the other three stop immediately. "It might be best if you guys stay here—I'm not sure what kind of welcome I'll get when I step out there."

Mike Saderson frowned. "What do you mean? If it wasn't for you, we'd all probably be dead."

"Yeah, which was good for you, but another case could be made that Elliot and I started that bloodbath by not surrendering to the major, even though that would've probably meant we would all be dead right now and the entire village razed to the ground. Still, I should probably go out first, just to see how they react."

Calley Carter shook her head. "No way, we either stand together or fall separately."

Bolan glanced at Susanna Tatrow and Saderson, both of whom also had determined looks on their faces. "What about you two?"

Twin nods answered his question. "All right." Bolan slung his M-4 on his shoulder. "Calley, Mike, safe your weapons and sling them like mine. If we step out and the natives are hostile, stay together and move back into the brush. I'll cover your retreat, then we all hightail it into the jungle. Everyone got that?"

"Oh, God, not more running." Tatrow bent over and massaged her calves. "My feet are bloody hamburger as it is."

"Hopefully it won't come to that, Susanna, but let's be prepared, just in case. I just need to do one more thing, so everyone hold on a minute." Removing his night-vision goggles, Bolan inserted his earpiece and hit a speed-dial number on his cell phone. Turning away from the students, he gave the proper key word and was connected to HQ. "Stony Man, this is Striker, I need a translator program for the Huaorani language in the Amazon jungle, Ecuador."

The distant voice of Akira Tokaido thousands of miles away replied in an instant. "One moment, Striker. Jeez, you sure like to throw me a challenge, don't you?"

"Do you have one or not?"

"All right, all right, I have a program ready for you—it might be a bit rough, though. Just subvocalize the words you want to say, and you'll hear the appropriate translation, which you can then repeat. Good luck, Striker."

"Thanks. The program also translates overheard conversation, right?"

"To the best of its ability. It helps if the speaker is clear and not too far away—our supercomputers are good, but even they have limits, you know."

"Right, it'll have to do. Striker out." Bolan made sure his

earpiece was secure, then turned to the others. "Everyone ready? Here we go."

Keeping his hands low and away from his sides, Bolan stepped out from behind the tree and walked into the clearing. At first, no one seemed to notice him, then one of the villagers on the outskirts let out a surprised shout and pointed as he slowly came closer.

As one, the main group of men and women turned and looked at him. No one spoke, and even the crying children quieted down, as if they were also curious as to what had attracted everyone's attention.

Bolan kept walking slowly into the clearing, hearing the footsteps of the students behind him. Careful not to make any sudden moves, he raised his right hand.

No one answered or waved in reply, they all just kept staring at him. Bolan kept moving, the villagers parting for him as he walked closer to the center of the group. Several women, all of them sobbing, were clustered around prostrate, motionless forms. When one of the women spotted Bolan, all of them straightened and regarded him with the same unblinking stare.

"Okay, what now?" Saderson whispered.

"I don't suppose any of you happen to speak the native dialect?"

"Sure, the kids taught me the local curse words yesterday," Carter replied. "What about you?"

"I speak French and passable Portuguese, but nothing even close to what I'd need to talk to them right now, unfortunately. Okay, here goes nothing." Bolan cleared his throat and addressed the group, saying the words under his breath so the sophisticated translator program could "hear" them and give him the translated phrases—maybe they'd think he was just fumbling for the words. "Hello...we need to check the rest of...the village and...see if anyone...is still alive."

For a moment, complete silence reigned. Then, like a dam bursting, all of the villagers spoke at once, some of them jabbering angrily and gesturing at him, others arguing among themselves, still others waving at the village or the motionless figure lying on a cot. Bolan waited for the program to come back with whatever the villagers were saying, but all he heard was an electronic tone and a computerized voice. "Unable to translate phrases. Do you wish to try again?"

He had no idea what to do next.

"Hey, isn't that Etienne?" Saderson said.

Bolan followed Saderson's pointing finger and saw a limp form on the cot. "Yes!" Shouldering his way through the crowd, Bolan knelt by the man's side. The villagers' conversations took on an ominous tone as they crowded around Bolan.

"Guys, help me out here." He subvocalized again, then spoke the unfamiliar dialect loudly. "People, listen to me...I can awaken this man... Just a moment..." With what he thought was a suitable flourish, Bolan produced a small white pill and placed it under Etienne's tongue. The medicine was another specialty from the Department of Defense's research labs, a powerful universal stimulant that would counteract any tranquilizer in the subject's system.

Just as he inserted the pill, Bolan felt hands grab his shoulders and wrists and pull him away from the prostrate man. "No, wait...I can help him..."

The villagers grew angrier, holding Bolan firmly as they pushed him away from Etienne. They were so close and so many that he couldn't free himself. Bolan looked to the volunteers for help, but found them hemmed in on all sides by more villagers, one of whom was reaching for Saderson's slung assault rifle.

"No! Stop!" Bolan twisted out of the hold of one of the natives and grabbed his own rifle, intending to use it as a club if he had to, before a groggy voice made everyone pause.

"What in the *hell* is going on here?"

All heads turned to see a sleepy-eyed Etienne sit up, rubbing his face with one hand. He addressed the crowd in what sounded like a suitably admonishing tone, then waved at some of the younger men to help him to his feet. Men and women clustered around him, each clamoring for his attention. Finally, Etienne held up his hands and quieted everyone.

"I asked them what they were doing to our honored guests. So far I've heard something about soldiers taking over the village, Nancy being taken somewhere and guns—lots of guns..." His voice trailed off as he noticed the weapons Bolan and Saderson carried. "Perhaps I should be asking you two what the hell is going on."

"Uh, well, things have gotten way out of hand in the last hour or so." Bolan filled him in on what had happened, including the tranquilizers, adding that he'd thought they would help Nancy and he rest better after what they'd seen at the other village. "Now Nancy's been taken by the Colombian Army, which seems to be heading deeper into the jungle instead of back to a town with a jail, and there are dead and wounded people here that need help right away."

Etienne listened to the story, a frown darkening his face as other villagers spoke to him at the same time, gesturing angrily at the group of volunteers and particularly at Bolan. "They're saying that the major asked Nancy, you and the other man to surrender. Nancy did, but you two did not. Why?"

"I—we—couldn't. I couldn't take the chance of all of us being killed or held for ransom. Look, the other villagers may not have long to live. You can ask me all of the questions you want, but minutes we can't spare are ticking away for them right now."

Etienne regarded him for a long moment, then nodded. "You and I will speak later." He turned to the villagers and rattled off commands, sending groups scurrying to different parts of the village. When most of them had been dispersed, he turned back to the volunteers. "Do any of you have medical training?"

Bolan and Tatrow raised their hands, with Bolan speaking first. "I've cared for wounded people before. Susanna?"

"I'd almost finished my paramedic course in Oxford before coming here." The stocky Britisher tried to hold everyone's surprised stares. "What, I just felt it wasn't for me, that's all."

"All right, Susanna, you're on triage. Bolan, you assist. Calley and Mike, you help with whatever needs doing. Where's Tom and Paul?"

Saderson's voice almost cracked, but he cleared his throat and continued. "They…they didn't make it."

Etienne walked over and clapped him on the shoulder. "I'm sorry to hear that. We will grieve for both of them later, but right now the living need us more. Let's get to work!"

THE NEXT THREE HOURS were spent diagnosing the various wounded, thirteen in all, and cannibalizing every medical kit they could find, including some of the veterinary medicine. As Bolan told Tatrow, "Penicillin is penicillin, no matter if it's supposed to be for a dog or a human."

As much as Bolan wanted to go after Kelleson and Morgan, he also knew he couldn't just leave these innocents in the lurch. If they'd wanted her dead, they would have killed her already, he realized. I have to make this right before I leave—I owe them that much.

The final count was eight dead and fourteen wounded. Unfortunately they couldn't save everyone, losing two in the treatment process, including one of the women Bolan had helped make breakfast with the day before. She'd bled out through what Bolan and Tatrow had thought was a relatively minor wound, but which had turned bad in a heartbeat. She had quietly passed away while they'd struggled to tie off her ruptured artery, ending up with their hands and forearms covered in blood and Carter quietly throwing up outside. Susanna sat back on her haunches in Kelleson's hut, which they'd transformed into a makeshift infirmary, tears streaming down her face.

Bolan knew exactly how she felt, but he washed his hands in hot water and motioned for her to do the same. "You did everything you could, and we've got more people that need our help. Now come on."

She had glared at him with such a venomous look Bolan thought he was about to get slapped, but without a word she brushed by him and scrubbed up for the next person.

At last, all of the injured had been stabilized enough until medical professionals could see them, but the tally had been costly. Bolan figured at least four or five would end up with crippling injuries, and he knew there would be children here who would grow up minus a limb long after he was gone. The rest of the villagers seemed to accept this more stoically, and as he worked, Bolan noticed more than one native who was missing a couple of fingers here, half a foot there, others even their entire lower limb. They compensated with ease, however, so much so that he hadn't really noticed it until then.

After the last victim had been taken care of, Tatrow and Bolan supervised the cleaning of the hut, then she had staggered off to bed. Bolan, on the other hand, figured on being up for a good long time yet.

He went to find Etienne, who was overseeing the burial detail. The men and woman had prepared graves for their kinsmen, and the entire village had gathered to pray over the bodies, each wrapped in white cloth, all the village could afford. Etienne stood at the head of the row of graves, head bowed, tears streaming down his cheeks.

Bolan stood off to the side, having no desire to interrupt the solemn ceremony. He had already intruded enough on the victims by snapping surreptitious pictures of each one as evidence of what had happened to them. Unfortunately, he presently had plenty of time to reflect on what had happened here and his part in it. *If it hadn't been for Morgan and me, these people would probably still be alive,* he thought. Bolan knew thoughts like these were supposed to be avoided, since they distracted him from his mission, but he couldn't help considering it as he waited.

The brief service was over quickly, and villagers began shoveling dirt into the graves. Etienne consoled family members who had lost relatives or children, staying at the gravesites until theirs were filled in. Bolan knew they would have to be guarded for the next few days, to keep animals from digging up the remains.

At last Etienne had finished ministering to the villagers and approached Bolan. "I appreciate all you've done here today."

"What choice did I have?" Bolan looked around at the village, the huts ripped apart by bullet holes, the earth torn up by the wheels of the APC and dark spots on the ground where people had been shot and bled to death. "I had to try to fix what I helped cause. Where are Tom's and Paul's bodies?"

"They have been wrapped and placed in suitable containers. The elders have contacted the Red Cross station at Nueva Loja, and they are on their way here to assist us. They should arrive sometime in the next day or so and will arrange for the bodies to be shipped home." Etienne wiped his eyes and fixed Bolan with a steady stare. "What do you plan to do now?"

"I know where the major's taken Nancy—and I think they might have captured Elliot, too. I'm going after them. I thought you might want to come along."

"Yes, I do wish to come along. I'll prepare the Rover." Etienne started to walk away, but was stopped by Bolan.

"You need to know that I'm not going there to negotiate or ransom her back. I will do what's necessary to get her back."

"Are you planning to go up against the Colombian Army?"

"Hopefully not, but I will if I have to. With any luck they'll have stopped somewhere, and I can do my own kind of negotiating with them—it starts with a bullet and goes up from there."

"I'd better grab that rifle from Mike, then, shouldn't I?"

Bolan nodded. "Yeah, it just might come in handy. We're leaving in ten minutes."

## 22

Bolan drove as fast as he dared down the rutted dirt road, the Range Rover scraping bottom every few yards as they jounced along the narrow lane. He kept an eye on the display on his cell phone, which showed the decreasing distance to the small bug he'd planted on the Urutu.

In the passenger seat, Etienne braced himself against the window frame, swaying back and forth with the erratic vehicle with the ease of years of practice. He hadn't said a word since they'd headed out, instead divided his gaze between the road and Bolan's face.

They had just finished packing when Saderson ran up to Bolan, asking to go with the men. Bolan had said no, and left no room for argument, telling the college student that his place was at the village, not with them. Ever since then, he'd felt Etienne's gaze on him, not accusing or condemning, but more as if he was evaluating him. Bolan didn't mind—he'd been under more intense scrutiny before.

"Better slow down, the road doglegs right here, and it can send you into the bush if you're not careful."

"Thanks, I probably should have had you drive in the first place." For the tenth time, his eyes flicked to the back, where their meager arsenal of weapons lay—the two Colt Commandos, two Galil assault rifles that had been left at the village. Bolan's pistol was holstered on his hip. The other sniper's weapon had been rendered inoperable by the hail of machine gun fire that had killed its owner.

Bolan had given the pistol from the soldier he'd killed in the tent to Tatrow, advising her to keep it hidden unless the situation turned critical, and left a Galil ACE with Saderson with similar instructions. He had been torn about taking the rest of the weapons, but leaving them might have caused the Colombian Army to crack down harder on the villagers. Besides, Bolan and Etienne would no doubt need to use them, as well, since both Colts used 5.56 mm ammunition, which could be a life-saving feature.

As they came around the bend, Bolan hit the brakes. A large jaguar crouched in the road, sniffing at a patch of dirt. Bolan brought the Rover to a stop and drew his pistol.

"What are you doing?"

"I want to see what it's smelling." Bolan rolled down his window just enough to stick the pistol out. Keeping an eye on the big jungle cat, he fired a round, making the predator start and bound into the underbrush. "Let's go."

Etienne picked up the Colt Commando and made sure there was a round in the chamber. He hit the release on the sunroof, waiting for it to retract before standing. "Go look, I'll cover you from here. I should warn you, however, that if that jaguar comes back, he can probably leap from a tree on either side of us and break your neck before I could fire."

"Guess I'll have to take that chance." Watching the nearby jungle in case anything came charging at him, Bolan opened the SUV's door just wide enough to slip out, leading with his pistol. Keeping his back against the fender of the Range Rover, he walked to the front of the vehicle, then out to the dark spot the jaguar had been sniffing and knelt beside it. Running his hand over the packed dirt, he sniffed his fingers. He examined the tracks in the bottom of the rut, too, then rose to his feet and ran back to the SUV. Jumping in, he slammed the door and got the Rover moving again as Etienne sat down and closed the sunroof.

"Blood, pretty fresh, maybe a couple of hours old. The

tracks in the ruts look recent, as well. We're definitely heading in the right direction."

"Good." Etienne flipped the safety switch on the assault rifle and returned it to the back, then watched Bolan for the next few miles. Finally, he spoke. "Why didn't you surrender when the major requested it?"

It was Bolan's turn to regard Etienne for several long seconds. "As you've probably guessed by now, I'm not one of the usual volunteers and I'm not a journalist, either. I work for a nongovernmental organization, as well, but it's the complete opposite of SARE."

"What do you do for this organization?"

"I'm sent to troubleshoot situations around the world. They placed me here to make sure nothing funny was going on before the oil companies came in, and set me up in your village. No one here was aware of my real mission, not even Nancy. I think she can help, however, which is why I'm going after her. I couldn't surrender to Medina because he probably would have hauled all of us off to jail, leaving the rest of you defenseless against whatever's going on out here. It was never my intention to have innocent people caught in the cross fire, but that second group of mystery men started shooting while I was trying to get the volunteers out, and everything just went to hell from there. Anything else you'd like to know?"

"No, you answered the rest of my questions already, and I appreciate your honesty. Do you think the Colombian Army is behind all of this?"

Bolan shook his head. "It doesn't make any sense. They're spread thin as it is out here, and they simply don't have the capacity to engineer something like this. They'd just charge in and kill the villagers themselves if that had been their goal."

Etienne digested this for a moment. "So you think the second group was behind the slaughter at the village?"

"Right now, it's the only theory that makes any sense, although I still don't know why yet. The guerilla activity in the area has quieted down, although I'm aware of any number of factions that could erupt at any moment. But, the assault was done with a very specific goal in mind—eradicate anything moving."

Etienne gazed out the window at the dark jungle flashing by. "I had relatives there—cousins, but family regardless. The idea of someone just coming in and slaughtering them outright makes me want to…" His voice trailed off, and for a moment Bolan thought he might be crying. "It makes me want to kill whoever did this."

Bolan marked their position on his phone's GPS program, then gunned the Rover's engine, powering the SUV out of the ruts and over the side of the road. "Well, you just might get your chance. Looks like they've stopped about a mile up the road. We go in on foot from here."

Checking for jaguars or snakes both in the trees or on the ground, Bolan got out of the Rover and retrieved his M-4 from the back, checking the magazine and ensuring that the weapon was ready to fire. He also stuffed the two extra mags into his cargo pockets.

Etienne armed himself with the Colt Commando carbine and a spare magazine. Bolan handed him a full canteen and took one himself. He also handed Etienne a stubby machete, keeping another, and one of the two smoke grenades he had taken from the dead mercenary. He grabbed his night-vision goggles, ensuring its small battery pack was fully charged.

Etienne pulled back the cocking lever on the Colt, jacking a shell into the chamber. "I assume you've come up with a plan during the drive."

"Naturally, although it has a lot of risk. Basically, we'll split up and approach through the jungle from separate directions. I'll see if I can get Nancy and Elliot free, while you try to reach the 12.7 mm machine gun, then you can cover me until we get to the Urutu and drive right out of here."

Etienne nodded. "What happens if we're discovered?"

"If they open up on us, pop smoke and head back to the Rover. If you beat me there, set up a position that lets you see down the road, both ways if possible. I'll disengage and follow behind. If I'm not back in ten minutes, I'm either dead or captured, and you're on your own. If you get Nancy free, your primary mission is to get her and you out of here ASAP."

Etienne smiled again. "Which one of us gets the keys to the Rover?"

Bolan tossed them to the short man, who caught the ring in one hand. "Better you take them, you'll probably be able to withdraw more easily. Also, take this." He tossed the other man his cell phone and earpiece. "It's set to vibrate, just tap the earpiece to pick up the call. If you need to call me, just say *Striker, go,* and I'll get buzzed." Bolan pulled his night-vision goggles down over his eyes. "Ready?"

Etienne inserted the earpiece and shoved the phone into his pocket. "Absolutely."

"All right. I've plotted the best course to the site, so I'll take point—"

"Actually, I think it'd be better if I took the lead. If we come across the team, I might be able to convince them to only capture me, but you—" he waved at Bolan in his mottled clothes and NVGs, making him look like an invader from some ill-defined but violent future "—you'd probably get shot on sight. Besides, I can clear a trail better than you."

Bolan had been about to protest that the thermal vision sensor in his headgear would alert him to any ambush, but closed his mouth and motioned at Etienne to go ahead. "Lay on, MacDuff."

"And damned be he that first cries, 'hold, enough!'" the short man replied as he melted into the undergrowth.

Bolan followed, assault rifle at the ready.

**23**

In his element again, Bolan followed the short man through the thick jungle with ease. Etienne moved like a brown wraith through the night-black forest, his machete flicking out to cut a vine or clear a branch with minimum effort, creating a well-defined but natural trail through the underbrush.

Within ten minutes, they'd covered the ground between them and the enemy camp and crouched at the edge of a large clearing, Bolan turning off his goggles, as there was plenty of light to see by. He reached into a thigh pocket and took out the Semtex charge that he'd retrieved from the volunteer tent. They watched the activity in the clearing—camouflage-dressed men with slung rifles smoking and laughing as they relaxed. The guards looked professional, but Bolan spotted gaps in their circuits that he could exploit if necessary. He counted ten visible men and allowed for a possible half dozen more inside the rest of the tents.

Switching his goggles to thermal vision, Bolan scanned the campsite again. "Nancy and Elliot are being held in that large tent at the back, on the far side opposite the generators," Bolan whispered. "I'm going to circle around and plant this charge on the generators, then move to free those two. Save your night vision—the signal to move on the APC will be when I blow the charge."

"All right." Etienne hunkered down to wait.

"You want this?" Bolan offered his silenced pistol, butt first.

Etienne shook his head and held up his razor-sharp machete. "I have my own silent weapon."

"All right. Remember, wait for the explosion."

"I will."

Bolan melted into the underbrush, machete in one hand, silenced pistol in the other. He didn't hurry—it was obvious that the men weren't going anywhere, and he needed to make sure that he wasn't discovered until he could free Kelleson and Morgan.

The clearing was large, and going around it took time, but eventually Bolan reached the generator hut. He used his Leatherman to unscrew a corrugated panel at the back, then slipped inside and set his charge on the main generator, making sure to disable the backup before leaving. He crawled out and replaced the panel, then headed for the large tent where Kelleson and Morgan were being held prisoner.

Within minutes, he was behind the tent. Switching his night-vision goggles to thermal vision again, he saw two seated figures between two standing ones holding long black rifles. Two other people were in the tent, as well—a tall man who paced back and forth and a short man who was standing much too close to one of the seated figures. Bolan could hear voices from inside.

"Look, mates, this can go down hard, or it can go down easy. You pick easy, you just tell us everything you know about what you saw. You pick hard, and we're gonna find out everything you know anyway, it's just gonna hurt a hell of a lot more. Now which will it be?"

Bolan took a step back and raised his pistol, holding it steady in one hand, aiming at the standing guard on the left. With his other hand, he hit his sat phone, triggering the Semtex.

There was a loud *crack,* and the entire camp was plunged into darkness. At the same time, Bolan squeezed the trigger on his pistol and saw the first guard go down. He quickly adjusted his aim to the second man and fired, taking him down, as well. Bolan dropped flat as a burst of automatic weapons fire stitched a row of holes in the back wall of the tent while confused shouting reigned inside as different voices struggled to restore order.

Suddenly the figures inside were all moving chaotically, and Bolan was unable to make out friend from foe anymore. They all seemed to be leaving the tent, however—something he didn't want to happen.

Cutting around to the side, he saw a tall man in clean outdoor wear dragging Kelleson toward the APC, with a shorter man pushing Morgan ahead of him, as well. Gunfire erupted by the APC, making the tall man panic and run. Suddenly free, Kelleson tried making a break for it, but was captured by one of the other mercenaries and brought back to the APC. Bolan lined up his pistol sights on the shorter man, but he disappeared around the side of the APC, with Morgan as his hostage.

A figure appeared on the 12.7 mm machine gun and began blasting lead into anything that moved in the clearing, the heavy machine gun's throaty roar drowning out other shouts and gunfire. Bolan hit the dirt as a stream of bullets blasted apart the tent he was hiding behind.

Bolan unslung his M-4 and began taking out other enemies, putting them down with efficient bursts. In the back of his mind he was hoping Etienne was catching some of these shooters.

The machine gun suddenly fell silent and Bolan glanced up to see that Etienne had disappeared from the open turret. The Urutu's engine fired up, and the vehicle lurched forward, planning to use the clearing to turn around in.

Slinging his rifle, Bolan waited until the APC was close to him, then launched himself at it, trying to stay out of the line of sight of the windows until he reached the back of the personnel carrier. He leaped up and grabbed the back edge just as the large vehicle took off, accelerating toward the narrow trail it had made in the rainforest. Bolan pulled himself onto the roof, flattening his body against it as the APC picked up speed. The driver hit the gas again, making Bolan lurch toward the back edge of the roof, bracing himself just before he would have fallen off.

Checking his grenades, he found two smoke and one tear gas. His plan was simple: get to the top hatch, chuck all three inside and wait for the APC to stop. Once everyone inside spilled out, he would take all of them prisoner and sort out who was who later.

The Urutu slewed back and forth on the narrow jungle road, impeding Bolan's crawl toward the forward hatch. He was only a yard away when it flipped open, nearly crushing his fingers as it slammed into the roof. The muzzle of a Galil assault rifle poked out, inches away from his face. Bolan grabbed the barrel and wrenched it up and away from his head.

"Feckin' *doos!*" The small, wiry man Bolan had seen earlier popped through the opening, straining to line up the rifle with his enemy's head and pull the trigger. The two men struggled for control of the rifle for several seconds, neither able to get an advantage. The man squeezed the trigger, his weapon erupted in flame and spitting lead.

The merc suddenly leaned back, going with Bolan's energy instead of resisting. Caught off guard, Bolan fell forward, but pushed off the roof and slammed into the man, with the rifle trapped between them. He tried to move it up under the man's chin to choke him, but his opponent turned his head, letting the stock of the weapon scrape by his cheek. Still holding the gun by the grip, the shorter man's left hand shot to his chest, drew a wicked-looking dagger and thrust it at Bolan's stomach.

Bolan threw himself to one side, the blade slicing his fatigue shirt as it passed. He grabbed the man's knife wrist and twisted, trying to get him to drop the blade. Again they strained at both weapons, each attempting to get any edge he could. Bolan broke the stalemate by rearing his head back and slamming his forehead into the other man's face, feeling his nose break under the blow.

The mercenary shouted in pain and surprise, and Bolan used the distraction to haul himself back, releasing the knife hand but pulling on the rifle with all his strength. It popped free, but he staggered backward and fell on the roof as the Urutu slewed around a turn. Bolan's hand smacked against the roof and the rifle popped out of his grasp, sliding over the side.

"I'm gonna cut your *ballas* off and hang them on my wall, *trilkop!*" The man sprang out of the hatch and rushed at Bolan, whose hand shot down for the pistol on his hip, bringing it up to fire. Before he could line up his shot, the man lashed out with his booted foot, which connected with the pistol and sent it flying from Bolan's tingling fingers.

The man shook his head. "Not nice to bring a gun to a knife fight." He flipped the knife in the air and caught it, the blade pointing down to slash or stab. "Come on, get up!"

Bolan took his time getting to his feet, trying to come up with a plan that didn't end with him getting impaled on the end of the other man's knife. His rifle was still over his shoulder, but he knew he'd be dead before he could unsling it.

His opponent stepped forward, the dagger dancing through the air in a prelude to an attack.

Bolan stepped forward, as well, snapping his leg out in a hard, fast front kick to the man's chest. With a strangled grunt, he dropped his knife and stumbled backward—right into the open hatch. Instead of falling straight through, however, one leg went in, and he tumbled back down the sloped windshield of the Urutu to fall in the dirt right in front of it. Bolan didn't hear if he even got out a scream before the tires bumped over his body. He glanced back to see the mercenary's rolling body skid to a stop in the middle of the dusty road.

Turning back, he saw another guard inside the APC aiming a pistol at him through the hatch. Bolan hit the deck just as the guy fired, the bullets splitting the air where he had been a second earlier. Grabbing the tear-gas grenade, he yanked the pin and tossed it into the hatch, then followed it with both smoke grenades and slammed the top hatch shut just as the merc inside had put his hand on the edge to pull himself up. The high-pitched scream from inside was gratifying.

"Don't move!" The shouted command came from behind Bolan. Raising his hands, he turned to see another merc kneeling on the roof, his rifle pointing at Bolan's midsection. "Put your hands on your head right now!"

The gas should hit the driver right...about...now... Bolan braced himself and dropped to the roof as the Urutu suddenly braked hard. The merc was thrown forward, his rifle hitting the deck as he skidded toward Bolan. Grabbing the rifle barrel with both hands, Bolan jerked it out of the surprised guard's hands, then jabbed the butt into his face, stunning him. Another smack knocked him off the top of the APC, completely unconscious.

Bolan rose and stepped to the end of the Urutu, where coughing, choking figures staggered out of the vehicle. The camouflaged men waved their weapons around uselessly, unable to aim, or even see. Drawing his pistol, Bolan jumped down and went to work. Ten seconds later, all the remaining mercenaries were dead.

Kelleson and Morgan also came out, coughing and hacking. Bolan grabbed a canteen from each of the guards and handed one to each of them, standing back as they poured the water over their faces.

Morgan gargled a mouthful of water and spit it off to the side. "Kidnapped, beat up and teargassed, goddamn it! When I open my eyes, Cooper, you better be standing in front of me, and not some fucking local militia or rebels or something."

He cracked his swollen, red-rimmed eyes open, and Bolan returned the grateful smile. "What took you so goddamn long?"

Bolan was about to reply when Kelleson interrupted him. "Hey, where's the other guy—I think his name was Hachtman?"

## 24

Hachtman stumbled through the thick jungle, fending off low-hanging tree limbs and entangling plants with his arms. He had no idea where he was going, only that he had to put as much distance between himself and the people attacking the camp as possible. Once he was sure he'd lost them, he would figure out his next step.

The instant he'd seen the machine gun open fire on the mercs, Hachtman had released Kelleson and run for the cover of the forest, practically falling into the foliage. The moment he hit the ground he was up and running, tearing off into the undergrowth before that bastard who'd killed Kapleron could spot him.

As he slowed to a trot, Hachtman allowed a small smile to spread across his face as he remembered the surprised look on the mercenary's face as the heavy machine gun had torn the camp apart. He would savor that runty bastard's final expression for the rest of his life. Hachtman supposed that he owed whoever that man was his gratitude for removing that annoying thorn in his side. It was just as well, he supposed, this way he wouldn't have had to dress him down for accidentally capturing that oil company agent. However, he supposed, that also served its purpose. Perhaps he would be able to thank that man later—assuming, that is, that he got out of here in one piece.

Stopping to catch his breath. Hachtman wiped his face

with his sleeve and looked around, seeing nothing but thick, dark jungle in all directions. The situation was serious, but not critical, and Hachtman was not without resources. Pulling out his own sat phone, he accessed the web and pulled up his location, along with that of the nearest road, the one they'd been using for the past several days. It was roughly a half mile to the north-northwest and, using the electronic compass program in his phone, he determined the correct direction to go that would take him back to the road while minimizing his chances of running into his former prisoners.

Hachtman's tongue felt thick in his mouth, and he took out a small flashlight from a pocket of his vest and scanned for a water-bearing vine. When he saw one, he nodded in grudging acknowledgment at Kapleron's insistence that all personnel at the complex undergo a one-day basic jungle survival course. Taking a penknife out of his pocket, he slashed the hanging plant open and drank the clear liquid that dripped out. Somewhat refreshed, he rechecked his direction and began walking, wanting to cover as much distance as he could.

He trudged through the endless forest, his boots growing sodden and lumpy as they absorbed more water from the forest floor. He had been feeling his way along from tree to tree when he remembered the warnings they had all been given about snakes that lived in trees waiting for prey to walk by underneath. Suppressing a shudder, he decided to find a reptile-free tree to climb and wait until morning.

He was looking around for a suitable tree when he felt a sudden, crushing weight land on his shoulders, bearing him to the ground. Sharp, agonizing needles of pain stabbed through his shoulders and buttocks, and Hachtman felt hot breath, redolent of rotting meat, on the back of his head.

He had just opened his mouth to scream when the jaguar that had pounced on him sank its teeth into his neck, breaking it, severing his spinal cord and killing him instantly.

The jungle fell silent once again, broken by the occasional *snap* and *crunch* of the big cat settling down to feast on its kill.

## 25

Dressed in a colorful sky-blue and yellow printed sundress and broad-brimmed hat, Kelleson walked into the spacious lobby of the Hotel Araza. Greeting the concierge in fluent Portuguese, she was guided to the entrance of the hotel's restaurant.

The last twenty-four hours had been just as exhausting as the previous two months. Once the mercenaries had been eliminated, Bolan and Morgan had taken charge, located the nearest village and contacted both the Ecuadorian Army and the U.S. Embassy in Quito. Bolan had stuck with his story of being a freelance journalist in the wrong place at the wrong time. Morgan's Sulexco connection had served him very well, too, greasing the normally glacial wheels of South American justice and also ensuring that none of them were going to face charges over what had occurred.

The U.S. Embassy was sending a representative to investigate what had happened and also to try to defuse the rising tensions between Ecuador and Colombia. Bolan, however, was planning to be long gone before he arrived. But before he'd left the village, there had also been a tearful reunion and goodbye. Kelleson, Bolan and Morgan had attended the sorrowful funeral service for Etienne, who had been killed in the assault on the camp.

They'd also assisted with the recovery of Tom's and Paul's bodies, to be shipped back to the United States, and overseen statements taken from the surviving villagers about the attack. SARE had offered transportation for any of the remaining volunteers who wished to leave, but they'd all surprised Kelleson by expressing their desire to stay. Tatrow had put it best. "Now that the hired killers and soldiers are gone, perhaps we can get back to helping this village, like we were supposed to do in the first place."

Kelleson couldn't have agreed more. They had wanted her to stay on, as well, but she had told them that she just couldn't see the jungle with the same love that she'd had before the kidnapping and needed to take some time to come to terms with what had happened to her. "Who knows," she'd said with a broad smile. "I might return someday to check up on your progress, but right now I think the village is in very good hands."

Shivering a bit at the air-conditioning as she crossed the tiled floor, Kelleson smiled when she saw Bolan and Morgan deep in conversation at a teakwood table near a window with a splendid view of the rainforest. She greeted them both warmly, accepted Bolan's gallant pulling out of her chair— which he'd just beat a wincing Morgan to—and suggested a 2002 Ernie Els Bordeaux blend with dinner before perusing the menu.

"How are your ribs, Elliot?" Kelleson had noticed he was still a bit pale when she sat down.

"Better with each glass of wine," he replied. "Seriously, although I had three cracked ribs, fortunately nothing else was injured. I do still have to be careful about moving too fast, however." He grimaced as he switched position in his chair. "Like that, for example."

"And what were you two discussing so intently before I arrived?" she asked, her eyes mischievously flicking from the list of entrées to them.

The two men exchanged their usual inscrutable glances before Morgan replied, "Cooper had asked me what had happened while we were prisoners, and I had just finished telling him about the interrogation and beating."

"It was pretty scary." Kelleson took Bolan's hand, which rested on the table, hidden from Morgan's view behind the breadbasket. "I wanted to thank you again, personally—" she squeezed his fingers "—for coming after Elliot and myself. I didn't think we were going to get out of there alive."

Bolan sipped his wine to cover his surprise. "Well, I certainly couldn't leave you two in their hands. Probably never would have ever seen either of you again."

Kelleson nodded. "We might have found a way out, but with that many people around, I just couldn't be sure."

The conversation was interrupted by their waiter, who announced the night's specials and took their orders. Kelleson kept it simple, ordering roast chicken, while Morgan selected a roast leg of lamb, and Bolan went with a thick steak. Once the waiter had gone, Bolan leaned forward. "So, now that the mystery is solved, where are you headed after this, Elliot?"

"Probably back into the jungle to babysit out-of-shape engineers and listen to them bitch and moan about the heat, insects, food and everything else out here. You two might want to keep an eye on Sulexco's stock price in the next few months—if they find what they're looking for out there, the shares will explode."

"I'll keep that in mind. How about you, Nancy?"

"I've had enough jungle for a good long time, thank you. I would have liked to catch a flight out today, but the soonest they could book a seat for me was tomorrow, so it seems I'm fated to spend at least one more night in the Amazon." Kelleson stroked Bolan's hand again.

"I'm sure you'll find some way to pass the time before your flight leaves."

Kelleson looked at him while he spoke, but his face revealed no emotion whatsoever.

"What about you, Matt? You've sure got enough for a hell of an article—maybe even a book? What are your plans?" Kelleson asked.

"I've got to stop in Quito for one last interview, then it's back to the States to see what I can make out of this unbelievable adventure. One thing I'll never forget, however—meeting both of you." Bolan raised his glass. "To the two bravest people I've met in a long time."

They finished the second bottle of wine and had been listening to Morgan's tales of his non-classified exploits on behalf of Sulexco around the world when the entrées arrived. With the wine still flowing, it was an enjoyable, relaxed meal, their shared experiences creating a strange sense of camaraderie. They finished with fresh mango and guava sorbet and were enjoying cups of the strong coffee the hotel was known for when Morgan's phone vibrated.

"What the—that's the real problem with the time difference here—six hours earlier, they're still doing business in Washington. I'm afraid I have to cut this short, as they want me on a conference call at HQ." He flagged a waiter and motioned for the check. "Bill it to room 114 when it gets here, all right?"

"Elliot, we couldn't possibly do that—"

"Hey, what's the use of an expense account if you can't enjoy it once in a while? Besides, I haven't spent squat since I got here—we were stuck out in the freakin' jungle, remember? Relax, have another coffee, more dessert, whatever—it's on me." Morgan stood, took Kelleson's hand and kissed it, his face only betraying the barest hint of pain as he did so. "It's been a pleasure—very nice to meet you. If you ever decide to try your hand at private security, look me up."

He arched an eyebrow at Bolan. "Good working with you, as well. I expect our paths will cross again someday."

Bolan shook the proffered hand. "Who knows—it's a small world. Take care of yourself, Elliot, and thanks again."

The other man's expression turned serious. "No, thank you for saving my ass—and Nancy's—back there."

Tossing them both a jaunty wave, he strolled gingerly out of the restaurant, leaving Kelleson and Bolan staring after him. Swallowing the last of her coffee, Kelleson turned back to see Bolan gazing at her coolly. She smiled and reached for the decanter to refill her cup. "Quite a character, isn't he?"

"Yeah, you could say that." Bolan regarded her over the rim of his china.

Kelleson set her cup down and stared right back, trying to figure out exactly what his expression meant. "What?"

"I was just wondering—with this being your last night and all—whether you had any plans. I understand Nueva Loja can be a fun place after dark."

"Well, I had planned a quiet night in my room—alone. However, it is my last night in the country, and I could really use something to take my mind off what I—we've been through. Do you have any ideas?"

Bolan smiled. "Of course. Just let me take care of the bill, and we can go."

# Epilogue

Roldos awoke in the middle of the night with a growl in his stomach. Slipping out of his silk-sheeted king bed, he pulled on a silk robe and padded down his sweeping, grand staircase to the large entry foyer of his mansion, high in the hills overlooking Quito.

The palatial house was dark, the servants all finished for the night. Roldos crossed the marble floor, the Italian stone cool under his bare feet, and headed for the kitchen. Switching on the light, he walked straight to the massive, stainless-steel refrigerator, opened it and took out a quart of buttermilk. Reaching for a decanter of brandy and a crystal highball glass from in the cupboard above the fridge, he poured a generous dollop of the liquor into the glass, then filled it with buttermilk. He sipped it with a soft sigh.

"Hope you enjoy it."

The calm words made Roldos start, the glass slipping out of his hands to shatter on the tiled floor. He whirled to see a black-haired man with ice-blue eyes sitting at his kitchen island. He was dressed all in black, with some kind of strange harness on his chest, and held a pistol in his hand. Recovering his poise, Roldos drew himself up. "Who are you, and what are you doing in my home?"

The man shook his head. "Who I am isn't important. What I'm doing here is delivering a message. And don't bother shouting for your guards—they're indisposed at the moment."

His heart beating a little faster, Roldos shook his head. "Is this about that business in the Amazon? Hey, you go back to those *pendejos* at Paracor and tell them to hire better mercenaries next time. Outwitted by a bunch of college students and volunteers. Really..." He glanced at the man and his pistol, which hadn't wavered. "Look, it wasn't my fault. I delivered everything they wanted. You're pointing that at the wrong man. Put it down, have a drink, relax." While he talked, Roldos's mind raced. In the cabinet above his refrigerator was a .357 Magnum pistol. If he could just distract this guy long enough, he thought he could get it and shoot him. A simple home robbery gone wrong, that's how he'd explain it.

The man's next words chilled the businessman's blood. "I'm not from Paracor, but they'll be seeing me soon enough. Your buddy Hachtman left a treasure trove of incriminating evidence on his computer, and my superiors are reviewing it now. And in the next few days, there'll be one less PMC in business. But, that still leaves the question of what to do with you."

"Okay, wait—are you with the U.S. government? Santa Maria, why didn't you say so in the first place? What, you want a transfer down here, get you set up? I can pave your way into Quito on streets paved with gold—literally, my friend. Tell you what—let me get you a glass of brandy, and we can discuss this like gentlemen." Roldos turned back to his refrigerator—and the cabinet above it.

"Like you discussed your plans with the native Amazon tribes to slaughter them so greedy corporations could come in and rape the land? That sort of discussion?"

Roldos threw open the side door of the refrigerator and stepped behind it, hoping the steel would protect him as he scrabbled for the door to the cabinet to get his hidden pistol. He heard a strange *cough,* then another one, and felt a sharp pain bloom in his chest, followed by another one. Suddenly all the strength was flowing out of him, and his hand, although only inches from the cabinet door handle, just couldn't reach it. In fact, he was having a devil of a time simply standing....

Roldos slid down the counter to sit on the floor, his arms and legs no longer working. He tried to speak again, but only bloody bubbles came out of his mouth. He looked up to see the man in black standing above him.

He glanced at the refrigerator door, which now had two neat holes in it, then looked back down at the dying Roldos. "That kind of shit only works in the movies."

The man raised his pistol, so that Roldos was staring into its unblinking black eye. "You, my friend, have just signed your last crooked deal—ever."

Roldos saw a flash of orange-and-red fire, and then nothing more.

* * * * *

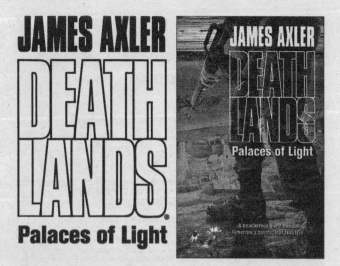